CLOUD JUDGEMENT

KAT WHEELER

CLOUD JUDGEMENT

KAT WHEELER

AUTHOR'S NOTE

All my readers... don't try this at home.

For Ben and Ken,
thank you for having such a good sense of humor
about all of this

CHAPTER ONE

FIRST TIME, LAST TIME

BEN Lang was in heaven. H-E-A-V-E-N. It was the best night *ever*. He begged his parents to let him stay home alone when the sitter didn't show up. After all, he was eleven years old. Almost a teenager. And certainly not a baby. He was allowed to walk home from school with his friends. That was much more dangerous than staying in his apartment by himself. I mean, c'mon. The building had a doorman. But he knew deep down that his parents only allowed it because it was so last minute, and the business dinner was very important to his father. Nobody had said anything to him, but he knew things were bad at his dad's work. He had heard things, grown-up things, when people thought he wasn't listening.

Since he couldn't count on it happening again, he vowed to make the most of his temporary freedom and do every single thing Tony Nitschke said he did when his parents went out. He made popcorn and streamed the new superhero movie his mom and dad hadn't let him see in the theater with his friends. So maybe he left the popcorn in the microwave a little too long and some of the kernels were a little overdone. It just added flavor. At least, that's what his dad said when it was his turn to make dinner and he burned it a bit. Covered in butter, it was still delicious.

And maybe the movie was a little too scary to have watched all by himself. He'd never admit it to Tony Nitschke when he saw him at school. No way.

He even took a sip of his parents' vodka from the liquor cabinet in his dad's office. It tasted awful and burned going down. But he wouldn't tell Tony that part either.

He cooked himself a pizza using the big pizza stone his mom always used in the oven all by himself. He again left his food in for way too long, and the kitchen got all smoky. The smoke detectors hadn't gone off, and he turned on the fan, so it couldn't have been that bad. Not really.

Tucked in his bed at the proper bedtime, because he just knew his parents would check the cameras in his room from their dinner, he could still faintly smell the smoke on his clothes. He thought if he just followed all their rules the first time they left him home alone, then they'd surely be willing to do it again.

Ben fell asleep content. *Best. Night. Ever.* And he never woke up again.

CHAPTER TWO

DESPERATE TIMES

I'VE got to get a new speaker guy.

Cameron Caldwell walked down the steps of her client's townhouse on the Upper East Side into the bright New York spring day. Turner was great. In the six months since she had started her consulting business, he had at times been a godsend. But for the love of God, if he played Diana Krall one more time during a demo, she might just slit her wrists. His demo routine was playing the same section of one song over and over again. Cameron shoved her earbuds in and cranked up the volume, hoping to replace the music playing on a loop in her brain. If she found herself humming that song later, she was going to kill him, and no one would blame her. A justifiable homicide if there ever was one.

But to be fair, he was at least less annoying than the lighting designers. On her last job, hearing about color warmth for hours on end almost drove her batty. She shivered at the flashback of the overly perky woman repeating "Isn't that white so warm? Don't you just love that warm white?" Ugh, cringe.

Taking a moment to savor the sunlight and freedom, she continued down Lexington Avenue. Cameron loved New York City. There was something about it. She didn't know whether it was the buildings, the people, or just the feel of it, but to her, it was a magical place. In her opinion, New York was the ultimate realization of what a city should be. It was loud and brash, but it could be so beautiful. The city was a never-ending mystery with so many different neighborhoods to explore. You could never get bored in New York. She loved every piece of it and couldn't imagine ever leaving.

It was a perfect spring day in the city, the kind people wrote poems about. Birds chirping, sun shining, and her morning meeting had gone well. Going into business for herself after getting fired from SmartTech was terrifying but was going reasonably well.

Well, it was going okay.

If okay meant she could sort of pay her mortgage, was burning through her savings, and was contemplating selling her shoes. Some of her best SmartTech customers had been passing her business, and her tenure as an A/V sales rep had helped get her off to a decent start. It was a feast-or-famine sort of thing, but closing this job meant she'd at least be able to cover her bills this month and eat.

Instead of selling SmartTech products to the audio/video dealers in New York City, she was now working with the end users directly. Counseling them on which products to buy and directing them to the right provider. It was a different perspective for sure, and sometimes the end users were more demanding than her dealers used to be. But she was her own boss, and as scary as it was, it could feel so rewarding.

Cameron had learned the benefits of being her own boss were mixed. In the positive column, she never had to be present in another one of Steve's terrifying quarterly sales meetings. On the negative, health insurance. Who knew premiums were so insane for the self-employed? But the best benefit was working when she pleased. Outside of scheduled client meetings, she was free to work on her own time. This worked out well for her, as she had never been a morning person. She could sleep in and do her work whenever the mood struck her. And on days like today, she could blow off the afternoon and head to the park. Or more specifically the farmers market. She was painfully aware that her cupboards were bare. It was her constant struggle. She was trying to be more fiscally responsible since she wasn't bringing in a fraction of the money she had been making at SmartTech. And saying the pay was sporadic was generous. She had vowed to quit ordering in for dinner, which any New Yorker knew was nearly impossible. Every restaurant delivered; it was a constant temptation. In a city with the best restaurants in the world, she'd had ramen noodles last night for dinner, and the night before. But it would be worth it if she could make her business a success. No number of Michelin-star meals could compare to that kind of freedom.

She'd squirreled away enough savings to get her started and had a few more months of cushioning before she really had to panic.

The problem was her apartment. Cameron lived in a great co-op building near Gramercy Park with a garage for her Jeep and a doorman. It was pricy but affordable on her SmartTech salary. At the time she bought it, Cameron thought of it as a great investment. Which it would be if she was still bringing in her salary, but getting fired had drastically changed her budget. Selling it wouldn't help; anyplace she paid rent in the city would still be expensive. No, the only way she would sell her place was if she left New York, and Cameron wasn't ready to do that. She just needed to keep working and make her business a success.

Pulling up her meal-planning app, she continued making her way to the subway, planning on heading down to Union Square and the outdoor farmers market there. It was, in her opinion, the best in the city, and if she felt like a real splurge after, she could head up a few blocks to Eataly and grab something as a snack while partaking in some of the best people watching in the city. Life couldn't be all pinching pennies and ramen noodles. You had to indulge every once in a while, no matter your circumstances.

One of the skills Cameron had developed after moving to New York was the ability to walk down the streets completely engrossed in her phone while dodging traffic and ignoring everything around her. It was, at times, a real-life game of *Frogger*. Her pace was typical New York, brisk, as she strode down the sidewalk. Moving swiftly while avoiding pedestrians and the random bags of trash that seemed to always litter the streets, she picked out recipes that auto aggregated into a shopping list. She was in her multitasking zone. Cam made a habit of never walking on the grates on the sidewalk and dodged them instinctively. She knew it was irrational, but she still maintained a healthy fear of falling through one. Something she would never share with anyone for fear of losing her street cred.

As engrossed as she was, it was still impossible to miss the line of three dark SUVs speeding up Lex and pulling off to the side of the street in front of her and parking. When the gleaming black door opened, a man was framed in the bright sunlight. She was momentarily stunned at the man who jumped out of the passenger seat of the middle vehicle with the grace of an Olympic athlete as he headed her way down the sunny avenue. Tall and broad-shouldered, he was maybe the best-looking man she'd ever seen in person. Dark suit, dark sunglasses, close-cropped hair; he looked like every film version of a government agent she had ever seen.

Yum, they must be shooting a movie here, Cameron thought absently. Meal planning and farmers markets were temporarily forgotten while she just took a minute to appreciate the view. It was the best Monday she'd had in a while. Closed a job, the afternoon off, and a show. So thrown by his good looks, it took her a second to notice that his trajectory wasn't going to steer him past her but right into her path. Crap, she better get out of the way. She didn't want to ruin or be in the shot. She watched him walk for a bit before she realized her first impression was wrong. They weren't shooting a movie; no cameras were around.

Must be the FBI. He really was exceptionally good-looking, she thought, watching him continue down the street. She continued to watch him powerfully stride her way, when she realized he was looking directly at her. Cam felt like a bunny a predator had just spotted in the woods. She had a moment where the fight-or-flight urge surged through her body, and she froze while contemplating running. A quick glance over his shoulder showed other similarly dressed men had gotten out of the other vehicles and were standing sentry. Running would be pointless. She wasn't fast; they could catch her if they wanted to. And why would she? She couldn't be in any trouble. She hadn't done anything close to illegal since the whole Synergistic incident last year that got her fired. So, she reigned in her anxiety and stopped walking. Shuffling herself out of the way of other pedestrians, she leaned a shoulder on the brick wall next to the entrance of a restaurant to wait. She'd know soon enough whether he was here for her or not.

She studied the men next to the SUVs while she waited and revised her second guess. This wasn't the FBI. The men guarding the vehicles were rougher, less corporate-looking than federal agents. They didn't have what she considered the standard short-haired, clean-cut look of the guy walking toward her that she associated with government suit types. Theirs were more scruffy faces, and they all looked like they needed a trim. Then again, she was basing her opinion on the limited experience she'd had dealing with the FBI after the HomeTech Hub situation. They had interviewed her every day she'd spent in the hospital recovering from her injuries. Well, that and watching movies.

No, these guys were different. The way these men moved, the way they looked uncomfortable in their suits, like they didn't quite fit. They reminded her of some of the guys she knew from back home. The ones who were constantly pulling on their collars whenever they had to get dressed up for a wedding or a funeral. Military, she was almost sure of it.

"Cameron Caldwell," the man said as he reached her. It wasn't a question. Pulling his sunglasses off his face. Wow, he had the longest eyelashes she'd ever seen. Thick and dark, almost black. For a moment, she was mesmerized.

Distance didn't lessen his attractiveness in the least. It was quite the opposite; the guy could be a model. Cover guy for *Badass Monthly*, or *I Killed a Tiger with my Bare Hand's* magazine. His voice just added to the package. Deep and rich, a warm, comforting tone. She hoped he was stupid. No one deserved to be that good-looking and smart.

"Yes?"

"Jack Rosado," he said, introducing himself, reaching out to shake her hand. Of course, he had a great handshake too. Firm and strong, but none of that crushing bullshit some guys tried to pull to prove how strong they were. She flashed back to her father telling her the true measure of a man could be taken with a handshake. She hoped he was wrong, or she would certainly be in for some trouble with Jack.

"I wonder if we could talk for a few minutes. I have a job offer for you," he said, gesturing to the middle car, a terse, quick motion that emphasized efficiency.

"You want me to get into a car with a group of what I can only assume are armed strangers? I don't think so," she replied, sliding to move around him and walk away.

"Ten grand for a consulting job. One day, two tops."

She stopped in her tracks. "You have an A/V job you need some help with?" she asked sarcastically, raising an eyebrow at him in disbelief.

"Of a fashion" was the answer, the expression on his face not changing a bit. She wouldn't want to play poker with this guy.

"Look, not to be rude, but I don't know you. I am not getting into a car and going to a secondary location with you. Didn't your parents teach you about stranger danger?"

"We have a mutual friend; Will Justus referred you to me."

Will. Of course, it was Will. It had been weeks since she'd heard from him. Wow, maybe months once she thought about it. Will Justus was an NYPD homicide detective that she'd worked with to try to find her friend Casey's murderer. They'd spent some time dating after their little adventure together. Trying to see if whatever was between them could turn into something. But it fizzled out over time. If he referred her, then this wasn't a typical consulting job. It would be something involving a crime, like the Synergistic incident. But that was obvious, of course; they didn't want her to design a system for them. But what did they want?

She flashed back to some of the moderately illegal things she'd done while pursuing her friend Casey's killer, and she knew.

The question was, did she want to get involved with this kind of thing again? She had almost died twice during the last incident. Could she handle that again? The promise of the ten thousand dollars weighed heavily on her mind. For two days' work? She could use the money. A relationship may not have worked out with Will, but she trusted him; he was a good man and a great detective. And really, how dangerous could it be?

"All right. Give me your driver's license."

"Excuse me?" His eyebrows furrowed incredulously, which somehow made him more attractive, giving a hint of personality to his stoic visage.

"I'm not getting in a car with a stranger without letting someone know where I am. Give me your ID. I'll text it to a friend, then I'll get in the car."

She thought she had blown her chance at ten grand when he just stared at her for a beat and resigned herself to no treat at Eataly and more ramen noodles in her future. But he slowly reached into his inside jacket pocket and removed a business card out of a case and handed it to her.

"I don't bring my ID when I'm on a job. Will this suffice?" He cocked his head at her with a slight grin. It appeared she had amused him.

She took the card from him and glanced at it. Two lines, no company. Just Jack Rosado and a phone number. No company, no email, not much at all.

She sighed, opened her phone, and snapped three pictures. One of his business card, one of Jack, and one of the SUV and the guys standing around them. She instantly sent a text to her old coworker Bill with the photos attached.

If something happens to me, it was these guys. If I don't call you in three hours, call the police.

"OK." She met his eyes and slid her phone in her back pocket as she handed him back his card. "We can go now."

CHAPTER THREE

THE JOB

JACK guided her to the middle SUV where he opened her door before he walked around and got into the back seat with her. It appeared he had good manners. No words were spoken between the men, but some hand gestures and nods from Jack had the other two vehicles loading up and pulling out into traffic.

"How do you know Will?" she asked as they moved to turn toward the FDR.

"We served together." Military, she was right. He handed her a crisp folder. "I work private security. My company was contracted to provide protection for a corporation. One of their executives and his whole family has gone missing. We'd like to see if you can provide any information that will help us find them."

My company; a corporation. Cameron noticed he was

being deliberately vague, but instead of confronting him, she just moved forward.

"He had a SmartTech system," she commented as she perused the first page of data in the folder. The SUV hit a bump on the road, and she had to clamp her hands around the paperwork to stabilize it. She'd wrinkled the edges on the top sheet. "You do know I don't work for SmartTech anymore. You could probably get more info by calling them directly."

"I'm aware of your employment status." He flashed a little smile. "Calling SmartTech directly would be problematic. We don't have time to jump through the necessary hoops to get the information we need. They've beefed up their security protocols in recent months."

Ah, so that was the source of the grin. That was probably her fault. The fallout from her actions the previous fall hadn't affected SmartTech directly. And their PR machine had managed to spin the incidents in their favor, but she had no doubt they'd still taken a hit. While the news outlets were creating explosive headlines claiming the HomeTech Hub was hacked, people became a little more suspicious of home technology for a time. It made sense Steve would fortify his security to shore up their liability. He didn't want to expose himself to potential negative press. Freakin' Steve.

"My bad," she said flippantly, which made him smile again.

"We were also told you had ways to get more information from their system than SmartTech would give us."

Will, damn him. Sharing secrets with his military buddy.

"I'll see what I can do." She glanced at the messenger bag, loaded with the gear she never left home without. Most women carried makeup in their purses; she carried cables and a Raspberry Pi. She felt confident that she could handle his request without any additional equipment. "Where are we going?"

"The house. We'd like to see what their system will tell us. They disappeared over the weekend, so their last movements are vague. We would like to narrow down the timeline. We want you to tell us about the last time the family was in the house and anything we may have missed."

"Ten grand for that?" she asked, meeting his eyes. It seemed like an absurd amount for such a small thing. "And then I'm out?"

"Yes. Tell us what you can. I'll deposit the money in your account and have a man take you home."

"OK, then," she answered, flipping through the file he gave her again, trying to smooth down the edges she'd crumpled. "Tell me what's in here, since I doubt I'll have time to go through the whole thing."

"We're heading to Brooklyn. The family lives in a townhouse in Williamsburg. Scott and Christina Nichols and their two boys Tayt and Jay. Ten and eight respectively. Christina's a stay-at-home mom. Scott works for the think tank we represent."

"What does he do for them?"

"Not sure" was his reply, so she put the pile of dead trees back in the folder, then half wedged it under her butt on the seat so they didn't fly everywhere. Cam reached into her bag to get her tablet while he continued talking. "He was at work on Friday. Business as usual. Left at the regular time. A neighbor saw him get home a little after six. No member of the family has been seen since. No alarms were raised until he didn't show up for work today. That's when his employer contacted us. We went to the house, did a cursory inspection. At first glance, nothing appears to be missing except one of their cars. We have people out now talking to more neighbors, the boys' school. Hopefully, something will pop up."

"Any ransom?" she asked absently, still searching on her tablet.

"Ransom?"

"I watch crime shows. Isn't there a window in which you can expect a ransom demand?"

He grinned in return. Seeing his full smile for the first time was devastating. Cute little dimples appeared on his tanned face. It didn't make him look any less tough but did add a hint of humanity to him.

"Not yet, which may not be significant. It depends on when they were taken. If it was Friday, it's problematic. Too much time has passed. If it was yesterday, we may still be in a reasonable window."

"Do you think they're dead?"

"There's no evidence of that in their house, so I'll proceed with the assumption they're still alive until I have a reason not to."

"Are the police involved?"

"Not yet. We'll reach out to them tonight after we've

done our initial investigation. Our employer has asked us to be discreet. At this point, we don't have anything to report. They may have left willingly."

"But you don't think so?"

"No, I don't. To pick up and leave with two kids takes a lot of stuff. There'd be evidence of that if they'd planned it. Things like clothes and suitcases missing. All their toothbrushes were still there. So were their cell phones and the wife's purse. There's a small possibility they left on their own, but if they did, they didn't plan it."

He was right, she thought. While a woman may leave the house without her purse on rare occasions, she definitely wouldn't leave her phone. And her limited experience with her nephews confirmed Jack's thought. Kids needed a lot of stuff. It'd be easy to tell if they'd packed for them.

"Virology," she said.

"What?" He turned back to her as they exited the Brooklyn Bridge.

"Virology," she repeated. "It's what Scott Nichols does for a living."

"How'd you find that?"

"It wasn't too hard. I just had to dig a little. He and his family have no social media presence. Which is odd. There should be something there. Stuff from when the parents were younger. School stuff from the boys at the bare minimum. That's significant. Everyone has a web presence. Even if it's just in relation to someone else. It implies they had someone scrub them. You might want to have someone check into that. He may have worked for the government at one time.

Or the think tank he works for may have government contracts now. I found an old paper he coauthored on the spread of infectious diseases. I just skimmed it, but it's pretty terrifying. Got email? I'll forward you the link."

He nodded and spelled it for her. Generic email domain. He wasn't giving anything away with that.

"Virology? Shit."

Shit indeed. Anybody who dealt with the study of viruses in the current climate, with biological warfare a constant threat, wasn't anyone to take lightly. This quick little job just got a hell of a lot weirder.

CHAPTER FOUR

THE NICHOLS HOME

THE Nichols had a beautiful brownstone in Williamsburg. Walking up to the front door, she couldn't even guess at what it would sell for. She clocked the alarm panel on the wall as she made her entrance into the house. Good, it was a brand that integrated well with SmartTech; that would make her job easier. Her mission, ever since her discovery in the car, was to get them whatever information she could as quickly as possible and get out. She needed money, not trouble. And Jack, good looks notwithstanding, was definitely trouble.

The second thing she noticed was that their house was immaculate. Super clean. How did you keep a house this clean with two kids in it?

"Did they have a housekeeper?" she asked, running her finger across the front of a bookshelf. No dust. Not a speck. The carpet looked brand-new. It even had vacuum lines visible on the surface.

"Yes, once a week. Comes on Tuesdays. So, they wouldn't have noticed their absence yet. Why?"

"It's really clean in here." She moved around the living room and into the kitchen. It was a completely open first-floor plan. "I mean super clean." She ran her hand across the granite countertops in the kitchen and leaned down to smell. Lemony fresh. "How could a house with two children under ten stay this clean for almost a week? Would kidnappers clean up after themselves?"

Jack looked around the space with new interest. A few quiet words to two of his guys had them moving throughout the rest of the house. She assumed to check out the other rooms on other floors. She had tallied his team when they'd gotten to the house. Two guys in the lead car, one other with her and Jack in the middle, and four guys following in the rear car. Those four had stayed outside when they'd gone in, leaving her on the first floor with Jack and one other man. He didn't seem inclined to introduce her to the rest of the team. That was OK. She wasn't there to make friends. She could focus, do her job, and get out.

"Where's their equipment rack?"

"This way," he said, leading her to a staircase hidden behind a column in the living room. He led her down to a basement with a playroom and an office to the side. Just past the office, he opened a door to the mechanical room.

The tiny space was cramped and unfinished, dirty in that way old concrete tended to be. Like the dirt had seeped in and became ingrained in the floor forever. There was creepy silence in the house, as if it had been abandoned. Or maybe they just had good soundproofing. Leaving the door open to avoid getting claustrophobic, she walked to the equipment rack. A thin layer of dust covered everything down there. Guess the housekeepers didn't clean this room. She looked at the gear for a minute, taking note of what products they had, before plopping down on the floor in front of it and reaching into her bag.

"Do you have their Wi-Fi info?"

"Yes," he said, passing her a Post-it.

IcanWiFitwiceashigh, cute. Someone in the house was a reader.

She pulled out her laptop and logged in.

"What are you looking for?" she asked, settling in and beginning to focus.

"Anything you can tell us that may narrow down the window of when they were taken. Anything at all about their last movements."

"Got it."

She pulled a cable and a flash drive out of her bag and prepared to work. Her first step was a network scan. That would tell her everything that was connected in the home and where she could look for answers. You just never knew what could be connected to someone's system. More and more devices were becoming internet capable these days, and information could be recovered from any one of them. She'd even seen a set of smart salt and pepper shakers once. Why anyone would need that, she couldn't imagine, but for the price Jack was paying her, she'd be thorough and explore everything.

While the scan was running, she grabbed another cord and plugged her laptop directly into the SmartTech processor. Steve may be trying to beef up security, but he couldn't stop this. Security measures only went so far. There was no stopping her when she was directly connected to the machine. She accessed the unit's hard drive and pulled all the records of the commands processed in the last week. That covered the window of their disappearance and then some.

"OK, looks like everything was fine until Friday night," she said to Jack, his partner next to him taking notes. "Tons of stuff being used all that night, TV, lights going on and off, etc. Lights off in one of the rooms at 9:36 p.m., so that's probably when the kids went to bed. Lights off to the rest of the house and security system armed a little after midnight. So that's probably when the parents went to sleep.

"Then nothing until the alarm is deactivated at 3:37 a.m. and the door to the garage at 4:08 a.m. That's it. No other activity until today. Front door entry at 9:16 a.m. I assume that's you and your team."

Jack appeared to be lost in thought at her words while the man next to him scribbled furiously and spoke to her for the first time.

"Garage door at what time again?"

"Not the garage door," she corrected, "the door that opens into the garage from the outside. Not as noisy as the big garage door. And it was 4:08," she replied. He nodded.

"Thank you," Jack said, looking at her again. "I'll have

the money deposited to your account and one of the guys drive you home now."

She could walk away. Get out of the situation right then. Cameron struggled briefly, internally debating whether to walk or not, but that was not her way. She couldn't leave a job half-finished.

"Not done yet," she commented with a grin and went back to her laptop.

"What else are you hoping to get?"

"No sure yet. Hang on a minute." Both men watched her diligently as she typed and clicked around on her laptop. The second man startled a bit when a sound came from the office next door. She could see him reflexively reach for the gun at his hip as he turned toward the sound.

"Chill out," she said, amused at his reaction. "It's just their printer. I'm getting you hard copies of all the data. OK, looks like they have cameras. All the recordings have been wiped, typical, but they didn't get the logs, just the videos. So, I can tell you that the camera over the garage was triggered at 3:32 a.m. Saturday. You may want to check that out. It's obviously where they got in. They disabled the surveillance system after that, so that's all I can tell you there."

At that, Jack picked up his phone and began texting. Probably to notify his team of the entry point. She scrolled back through the data the local area network scan had provided and didn't see anything else that stuck out as helpful. No weird devices attached to the system, but she sent a copy of the surveillance data to the printer for them anyway. There was no telling what would be useful to them later. She gave a subtle glace to Jack to make sure he couldn't see her screen and then saved a copy of everything she found to the flash drive she had with her and another copy to her cloud account. If previous experience had taught her anything, it was that you could never be too careful.

Once she was sure she'd seen everything there was to see, she closed down her gear and disconnected it from the system. As she packed up her bag, she directed the second man to go grab the printouts from the printer in the office next door and addressed Jack.

"That's it; that's all I can get for you."

"Thank you. It's more than what we had. Giving us the specific times of the abduction will allow us to narrow our search. We can now focus on when to pull traffic cam footage, etc. This will save us a ton of time."

"Worth ten grand?" she asked cheekily.

"A bargain." He smiled as they made their way back up the stairs to the main floor.

One of the guys who'd been riding in the front car, who she had been trying her best not to think of as Holey Moley due to the massive mole on his right cheek, walked in through a door in the kitchen that she could only assume led to the garage.

"You were right; that was the entry point. It's easy to overlook, which is why the guys missed it at first glance, but the outer door has scratches around the lock. It's faint, but it could be evidence of tampering. We're running tests to see if we can get any trace right now. It's difficult because that huge Marconi battery is in the way."

Cameron's ears perked up. "They have a Marconi?" Marconi's were the first and most high-tech electric cars on the market. They were highly coveted, and there was a long wait list to get one. If she ever decided to part with her Jeep or found herself in a position to have two cars, she was definitely getting a Marconi.

"Yes," Jack answered with a measured tone. "It's the car they left in. Don't get excited," he said at seeing her expression. "They disabled the tracking before they left."

"I doubt it." She was full-out grinning as she pulled up her bag and set it on the kitchen counter, then pulled out her laptop again.

"Explain." He leaned forward, crossing his arms on the countertop and encroaching on her space.

"Hang on. I'm checking to see which model they have."

"Brand-new Marconi, Flagship model. All the bells and whistles."

"Oh," she said, shoulders dropping. She was a little deflated about being beaten to the information. "Then, yes, you can probably get a location from it."

"How, if they disabled the tracking?"

"Those cars are basically all one big computer, and each component has its own tracking system. If your kidnappers didn't do their homework thoroughly, you may get lucky. Yes, there's a standard onboard GPS you can ping and get a location, and, yes, you can turn it off. But if that's all they did, you're golden. Everything else in that car has transmitters. Most newer-model cars send vehicle monitoring reports to users about the status of their cars. All that data comes from computers built into all the mechanics in the car. Even if they were smart enough to disable some of it, I highly doubt they could get all of it without rendering the car undrivable. If they drove out of here in that car, you've got a better than average shot at getting a location. You could probably ping the gas cap in that car and get a location." She smiled smugly, finally feeling like she'd earned that ten grand.

"So do it," Jack replied, making a testy shooing motion at her nonmovement.

"Oh, yeah, I can't do it," she answered, sheepishly. "You need information on the mechanics in the car to connect to it. You'll have to reach out to Marconi. They're the only people who'd have that information."

"Can't you get the information off the battery in the garage?" Jack asked, running his fingers through his hair, obviously frustrated.

"Um, no, each part has unique identifying information. And the car stuff would be separate from the battery. It's two different things; they aren't sold as a unit."

"Damn it, that will take forever. I can't even imagine the amount of bureaucracy it'll take to get them to release that information. They probably won't even do it without a court order. It'll take days if not weeks. The Nichols don't have that kind of time."

Cam knew he was right. Just because the information was available didn't mean it was easily accessed, and companies like Marconi had privacy agreements in place. Thinking about it, she realized they'd be lucky if it was weeks. A company like that may never hand over the information. And that realization made her sick to her stomach, because she knew what she had to do. It went against every instinct she had in her, but she couldn't just walk away. There were two little boys' lives at stake. How could she live with herself if she walked away all because she was scared to make a phone call?

"I… I… well, I may know someone who could help us out." Her stomach turned as she volunteered the information.

"Yeah?" His gaze sharpened on her, and she felt like all the air had gone out of the room.

"Yeah, I… um, well, I sort of know someone at Marconi. He may not help, but I can give him a call. Ask him at least."

"Ex-boyfriend?" Jack asked, noticing her reticence to make the call.

"No," she replied, swallowing, her throat suddenly dry. It was so much worse than that. "My brother."

CHAPTER FIVE

STRANGER DANGER

"YOUR brother works at Marconi?" Jack asked.

"Yeah," she replied. Still not moving or reaching for her phone.

"Call him."

"I'm going to," she answered, still unmoving. She felt stuck in place in front of her laptop, eyes unfocused, staring at nothing.

"Cameron," he said, his face softening, his voice lowering, as he sensed her discomfort with the task he'd asked of her. "I can see this is uncomfortable for you. But this situation is bigger than whatever is between you and your brother. Set it aside for the moment. People's lives are at risk here. Two little kids."

She sighed. "I know." And she did; calling Christian wouldn't be nearly as painful as how she would feel if she didn't try.

She reached for her phone. Scrolling through her contacts as Jack addressed Mole man. "It's time to bring in the cops. We now have confirmation this was an abduction. Call Will Justus at the tenth precinct. Tell him you work for me and what's happened. He'll find us someone friendly who covers this area."

"Will Justin?" Mole repeated incorrectly.

"No, Justice. J-U-S-T-I-C-E. Will Justice."

At that, Cameron froze momentarily. Her heart stopped beating, and she felt like time stopped. She had to force herself to continue to look through her contacts to find her brother's number. Justice, J-U-S-T-I-C-E. Jack was not a friend of Will's. Anyone who knew him knew he spelled his name with a U-S. Anyone. She'd heard him say it so many times when he met new people, and they commented on the irony of his last name. It's U-S, not I-C-E. Everyone who knew Will knew that. Someone who served with him would know how to spell his last name.

Holy shit, who were these guys? And what were they doing here, she wondered? Were the Nichols even kidnapped? Or were Jack and his team trying to track them down, and the Nichols had run on their own? Was she helping the bad guys? And if they were the bad guys, were they really going to let her go once she'd helped them?

She didn't know, couldn't answer those questions right then. She just knew she had to get out of there. And to do that, she had to buy herself some time.

CHAPTER SIX

CHRISTIAN CALDWELL

REALIZING   Jack, or whatever his name was, was finished addressing Mr. Mole and was back to focusing on her, she found her brother's name in her contact list and only hesitated briefly before hitting the call button. God help her, she was going to have to rely on her brother for help. She had to stop herself from crossing her fingers for luck that he was in a good mood. Even him picking up her call wasn't a certainty.

"CeeCee," he said when he answered. "To what do I owe this surprise? It's not my birthday or a major holiday. Mom said you got fired. Do you need money?"

What an asshole.

"Hi, Christian, how's it going?" she answered evenly, willing herself not to rise to the bait and engage with him. She needed his help, not a fight.

"Christian? Really? Now I know you need money. Shouldn't have gotten fired, kid. Maybe then you'd be able to take care of yourself. You wouldn't have to go running to your big brother for help."

"No, Chrissy, I do not need money. I need your help, so can you stop being a dick for five minutes?" And there it was. She could never hold her temper for long when talking to her brother. They brought out the absolute worst in each other.

"Here's a tip," he said, the amusement clear in his tone. "Calling me a dick isn't a good strategy if you're trying to get me to help you."

She ground her teeth and tried deep breathing to maintain calm. She was going to need a dentist after this conversation. She glanced up at Jack to see him staring at her. She had to pull it together and figure a way out of this; she couldn't let her relationship with her brother distract her. There were two children whose lives were at stake, and maybe, possibly, hers.

"I'm sorry, but look, I do need your help." She laid out for him her morning and how she found herself in the townhouse in Brooklyn. "So, my question is, is it possible to get a location from the car if they've turned off the location services?"

"Theoretically, sure, but it's illegal as hell, Cam. I'm sorry, but I just can't do it. I'd lose my job and quite possibly go to jail. You need to go to the police, get a warrant. I can help you expedite it, but that's it."

"C'mon, Chris, I know you can do it. This isn't about

me. Two little boys are missing here."

"I understand. That's why you need to call the police."

She started zoning out when he began going into detail on privacy laws and owner agreements. His lecture on responsibility may be on a different topic now, but it was one she'd heard a version of from him many times before. She was distracted by the man across the kitchen island from her. His eyes never left her, startling in their intensity. It felt as if he wasn't giving her any room to breathe. How was she going to let Chris know she needed help? And how was she going to get away from him long enough to come up with a way to sneak out of this place? He hadn't taken his eyes off her since they'd arrived. Finally, she just had to cut her brother off.

"I get it, Chrissy, you're scared. Liability issues or whatever. You don't want to lose your big fancy job. I knew I couldn't count on you. You're such a baby. That's why Dad would never take you to the gun range when we were kids, and he always took me."

"What are you talking about?" he answered, obviously confused. "It was the other way around. Dad didn't think girls needed to know how to shoot."

"I know." God, she thought, please let him get this. "The guys I'm with have already called the cops; I just need you to track the car."

"Cam, are you in trouble? Do you need me to call the cops?"

Hallelujah. Her brother may be an asshole, but he was super smart.

"Yes, exactly. How much time will it take you to see if you can get a location?"

"You need me to buy some time? Is someone there listening to you?"

"Obviously. That long? Surely you can get it quicker than that?" she replied. It was getting increasingly difficult to keep her conversations straight in her head. What she was trying to ask her brother to do versus what Jack would hear was starting to get complicated. She didn't want to slip up.

"OK, I've got you. I'll call the cops when we hang up. Just tell whoever you're with, it'll be a couple of hours."

"Gotcha. Thanks, Chris. I really appreciate this," she said. Meaning it in more ways than one.

"No problem, and, Cam, be careful."

She hung up the phone, setting it down softly by her laptop, hoping she could fool Jack for a little while longer.

She looked up at Jack and pasted on the most realistic smile she could manage. "He's going to do it."

"I heard. What now? We just wait and see what he comes up with?"

"That's about it, yeah. He should be able to ping something in the car and get you a location. He said it'd be a couple of hours at best. I've just got to send him the vehicle identification number," she answered, typing a quick email to her brother with the address of the house and the VIN number Jack had provided before shutting down her laptop and stashing it back in her bag. She didn't want to leave anything behind in case she got the opportunity to bolt. "You know it won't help much if they've ditched the car.

Which anyone with half a brain would do at the first chance they got."

"I know, but it might give us a place to start. In my line of work, more information is always a good thing. We could learn which direction they were headed and may be able to track them from there. At the very least, we'll be able to fill in more of their missing hours."

CHAPTER SEVEN

ESCAPE

IT was coming up on an hour since she'd spoken with her brother, and they'd moved into the living room to get more comfortable while they waited. She kept discreetly looking at her watch as they sat, killing time. She'd been visually tracking Jack's team, and for the most part, they'd left her and Jack alone. Preferring to walk around the perimeter of the property or explore other areas of the house. Cameron couldn't figure out why. Were they watching for other people interested in the house? She couldn't figure out what they might be looking for. The place was practically sterile, outside of the basement equipment room and the office she had seen, but she hadn't been upstairs to see the bedrooms. There were no family pictures on the walls, tables, or the mantle over the fireplace. No tchotchkes or knickknacks. The kitchen was spotless. How they kept a house with two kids this clean was beyond her. Her brother managed it, but he had live-in help. This didn't seem like that kind of place. The more likely answer was that they didn't. The whole thing could be a scam. Maybe there was no Nichols family. It would explain their lack of internet footprint. If that was true, then whose house was she in, and who were these guys looking for?

Another half-hour drifted by in agonizing slowness. Cam spent the time drumming her fingers on the soft upholstered armchair she'd settled in, shifting her weight, glancing around the room and freaking out. She'd never been a patient person, and judging by the looks Jack was giving her, he noticed as well. It wasn't much longer before she felt like she might have her opportunity. Holey Moley had been back checking in with Jack, and he sent him outside the house for the first time to join the others. Then Jack got up to use the restroom. It was the first time he'd left her alone since he'd picked her up. She quickly realized it might be the only chance she was going to get. She had to make her move.

She sat perfectly still for a full minute after he'd walked out of the room, counting Mississippis in her head. Then, as softly and quietly as she could manage, she slipped her messenger bag over her head and slinked over to the front door. It was flanked on either side by floor-to-ceiling windows. Peering out, she saw one of his men walking around the side of the house. With a quick scan of the rest of the small front yard, she verified her assumption: it was clear, and she was running out of time. How long would it take Jack to use the restroom? Men traditionally were pretty quick. She took a deep breath, made up her mind, and with no hesitation, she slid the door open and ran, leaving it wide open behind her.

Pumping her legs, she pushed herself as hard as she could to make it through the front gate. She wanted to breathe a sigh of relief when she made it out without anyone noticing her. At least that she could see. But she didn't stop, didn't take any time to get her bearings, she just hung a left, going against traffic, and ran. Weaving in and out of people, her bag banging against her leg with every step. When she reached the end of the block and at the first intersection, she finally stopped. Sucking in air, hands on her knees, she'd developed a stitch in her side. Looking up at the street signs, she had a decent idea of where she was but no idea where she needed to go.

She needed a place to get herself together and call for help. A police station? No way; she may have just been party to some criminal act, and until she had a clearer idea of what was going on, she wasn't going to present herself to the law. With her luck, she might be arrested. A friend's house? She had a few friends who lived in Brooklyn, but none close enough to where she was or who would be home in the middle of the workday. She needed somewhere nearby; she needed to get off the street. Standing up and putting her hands on top of her head, she began to pace, panting, trying to get her breath back from her sprint. She took a minute to look up and glance again at the street signs. She was on Jackson, and once she was static, she realized she recognized the butcher shop on the corner. She'd bought sweetbreads there once when a guy she was dating wanted to get fancy and try to cook offal. The meal was almost as bad as the relationship was.

The solution hit her like a lightning bolt. She knew where she was and where she should go for help. She was only two blocks away from Clint's shop. With a grin, she reoriented herself, took a deep breath, and took off running again.

Clint Bennett was a former customer of Cameron's, and one of the rare ones she truly missed. He was a bear of a man. Not just tall, he was at what she judged to be around six foot six, but wide as well. He had to be at least three hundred pounds, but she wouldn't have called him fat. More like thick or sturdy. And his larger-than-life personality matched his appearance. He was the kind of man who had a permanent grin and laughed frequently. He was a ton of fun at work events and meetings. He hid a raging alcohol dependency under the guise of being a wine connoisseur, and his predilection always guaranteed that at every business dinner they had, the wine pairings would be plentiful and fantastic. Most important to her current situation, he owned one of the few remaining brick-and-mortar audio/video shops in New York.

She burst through the doors of AV, Stereo, Design, Automation, and More—the unofficial but clear winner of the most obnoxious business name in the industry award—completely gassed out and sucking wind. The guy behind the counter must have been new, because she didn't recognize him, and he looked appalled at the state of her.

She was panting like a maniac, and her hair was sticking out everywhere. Her disheveled appearance did not fit in with the polished decor of the showroom. Or with the salesman she had startled with her jolting entrance. She always felt bad for the guys at Clint's shop because he required all of them to wear suits and ties when working the floor. It was exceedingly rare that any of the A/V nerds she knew ever seemed comfortable out of their typical T-shirts and jeans, and this guy was no different. Tall and stick-thin, he looked like a praying mantis. Long-limbed and bug-eyed, stuffed into an ill-fitting suit, he looked as uncomfortable as she felt. Like a kid playing dress-up in his dad's suit.

"Can I help you?" he asked hesitantly as she ambled her way over to him. He'd taken a half step back from the counter he stood behind, almost looking like he may try to run away from her at any moment.

She caught her reflection in the mirror and cringed. She was a bigger mess than she thought. She smoothed her hair back out of her face as she answered him, trying to regain some sense of propriety.

"Yeah, is Clint here?" she wheezed out, still trying to catch her breath.

"Sure," he replied. "Let me go see if he's available." He scurried quickly out of the room like he couldn't wait to be away from her.

As he walked away, she put her arms on the counter and laid her head down to rest. No doubt leaving smudges on the pristine marble countertop. That was it. She was finally getting herself a gym regimen. She'd told herself that multiple times during her incident with Synergistic but hadn't stuck to it. Well, this was the last straw. She wouldn't be caught unaware, running for her life again. She was getting her ass on a treadmill.

She made it. Jack must have discovered her missing; she had left the front door open after all. There'd be no mistaking that sign. Would he still be at the house? No, they would've bailed as soon as they realized she was gone. But the real question was, what the hell were they even doing there? Upon reflection, she was convinced that wasn't a family home. It was set up too much like you'd stage a property you were selling. No one lived there. And if that was the case, why did they need to check the electronics? Someone had been in residence in the house; that was for sure. She'd proved that with the data she found. Was that what they were doing? Trying to find someone who had been squatting on the property? No, there's no way a team like that would be called in for something so innocuous. They were a tougher group than that. Not investigators, they were all ex-military; she was sure of it. It was in the way that they carried themselves, the way they wore their weapons.

"Cameron? What the hell?" she heard from behind her and turned her head, still resting it on the countertop.

"Clint." She smiled gratefully, finally lifting herself off the counter and turning her body to face her friend. "I need your help."

CHAPTER EIGHT

GETTING THE BAND BACK TOGETHER

SHE was sprawled in a chair in front of Clint's desk when Will Justus walked in. Cam had her jacket off, sleeves rolled up, and her feet propped up on the edge of the desk, doing her best impersonation of a sloth, sprawled out in a most undignified manner. She was on her third bottle of water, and while she had gotten her breath back, her body ached. She felt like she'd just run a marathon, not just a few blocks.

It was her day to be making uncomfortable phone calls. Not only had Jack persuaded her to call her brother, but she had voluntarily called her ex-boyfriend. Her relationship with Detective Will Justus may not have worked out, but there wasn't anyone else she trusted to call in a pinch.

Upon her arrival at AVSDAM, Clint had taken one look at her appearance, pronounced that she looked like shit on a stick, and ushered her quickly back to his office. She didn't know whether it was for her benefit or because he didn't want any of the customers who might wander in the shop to see her.

His store had gone through so many iterations over the years. The majority of Cameron's old customers in the city had closed their retail and showroom spaces and gone to business offices only. Clint managed to avoid having to close shop like most of the others because he owned the building. His family had purchased the property over sixty years ago, and it had been handed down from generation to generation. Owning real estate in New York was an amazing advantage when trying to keep a storefront open when rent prices were becoming increasingly prohibitive. It was originally a smoke shop when his grandparents owned it, but you no longer could see any of that reflected in the store. Cameron did think she caught a faint whiff of smoke every so often, but that may have just been wishful thinking. She'd helped him renovate it a few years ago, and it became a super-modern and sleek retail experience that fit in perfectly with his gentrifying neighborhood.

He sat her down in an oversized leather chair and thrust a bottle of water at her, which she greedily gulped down. All Clint's furniture was oversized; she imagined it had to be to accommodate his hulking frame. She gave him the CliffsNotes version of what had happened to her in the last few hours, appropriated his desk, and pulled out her phone.

She called Will first; the most important thing was to get him on his way. The relationship between them was so undefined that as the phone rang, she was briefly concerned he wouldn't take her call. She shouldn't have worried. She told him she'd been kidnapped and gave him the address; she heard no hesitation before he said he was on his way and ended the call.

She then called her brother, who was sufficiently freaked out and on the other line with some vague NYC police department. He'd called several different precincts and tried to report her missing or get in touch with Will to no avail. Everyone he had spoken to had just blown him off. He'd been trying desperately since they'd last spoken, and his anxiety level was at an all-time high when she got through to him. She calmed him down, assured him she was OK and safe, and let him know she'd have Will reach out at a later date to get his side of the story. She'd had to beg him for a full five minutes before he agreed to not tell their mother what had happened. All she needed was for her mother to take an interest in what was going on.

Caroline May Caldwell, better known as Cricket, wasn't someone who was ignored. And if she caught wind of the situation Cameron had put herself in, she would have no peace for the foreseeable future, and she had enough on her plate at the moment. She shivered as she had a flashback of the last time she'd spoken to her mother. She'd never forget her biting comments when she told her she lost her job.

All my friends' children are all doctors and lawyers, and you can't even hold a job. I just don't know what to do with you.

Ugh, her family was a lot of work. They were uniquely capable of making her revert back to her thirteen-year-old self. Moody and confrontational. Hopefully, that would be the last she heard from them for a while, at least until the holidays when she could use alcohol as a socially acceptable crutch to endure it.

Will walked into Clint's office like he owned the place. He looked good. Just like she remembered. Not movie-star handsome like the mysterious Jack, but quietly attractive. His tousled brown hair and rumpled off-the-rack suit didn't do him justice. But Will didn't need anything to enhance his appearance. He was good-looking in a rugged, masculine way that appealed to Cameron. His presence was arresting, and she felt her heart give an extra little thump at the sight of him. She would have chosen him over pretty-boy Jack any day, no question. Guess that answered that: she still wasn't completely over him.

Looking at him, Cameron felt like no time had passed since they'd last seen each other. It was one of their more successful attempts at a date. They'd had dinner at the Irish pub by her apartment where they'd eaten the night they'd first met. They'd been able to finish their meal and had been walking back to her apartment before he'd been called back into work. The life of a homicide detective meant his time wasn't his own.

"Well, you look awfully comfortable for someone who's been kidnapped," he said, looking her over from head to toe. "No rope, no chains. This doesn't look like much of a kidnapping to me."

"Kidnapped may have been a strong word."

"I'm going to leave you guys to it," Clint said, apparently

reading the tension in the room and giving Will a hard stare as he made his way out of the office, shutting the door behind him. Somehow, she didn't think Will was impressed.

Will watched him go and slowly made his way to the desk and took the seat Clint had vacated. He crossed his arms on the desk and leaned forward. "OK, lay it out for me, then."

The words poured out of her. She told him of walking out of her appointment and meeting Jack, the trip to Brooklyn, the mysterious house, what she'd done while there, and her escape to Clint's.

"You got in a car with some random armed men just because he said he knew me?"

"It seemed legit. I took his picture and texted it to Bill," she replied, passing him her phone to show him the picture. "I was being safe."

He nodded, but she could tell he thought she'd been stupid. In hindsight, he was probably right.

"So, mercenaries, you think?"

"I think mercenaries may be a strong word too. Private security for sure; at least, that's what he said they did."

"This will go a lot faster if you'd stop exaggerating and just stick to the facts."

She imagined his head popping off. Sadly, she had never developed psychic powers.

"I'm so sorry, Will," she answered, leaning back in the chair and crossing her arms over her chest. "I'm just trying to give you the full picture. These are my impressions as it happened. Upon reflection, I have certainly developed a different opinion, but I don't want to leave anything out in case it may be important later."

"OK, do you think you can find the house?"

"Yes. It might take a little looking, but I can find it. It's not that far away." She watched as he nodded back. He was acting weird. So, the question became call him on it or not? Eh, she wasn't one for beating around the bush. "What's up with you? You're acting strange."

"Strange how?" he replied stiffly, straightening his spine. If he were a cat, she'd have said his hackles were raised.

"Oddly formal," she answered, giving him the side-eye.

His exhale seemed to take everything out of him, and he shook his head. His shoulder curled in, and his body seemed to deflate. A slow smile started to creep onto his face. "It's just... I mean, how do you keep getting yourself into these things?"

She looked to him, all ready to defend herself. But when she glanced up and looked at his expression, she couldn't do it. She burst out laughing. Will followed her, chuckling too.

"I just don't know what happened!" She wiped the tears from her eyes through her laughter. "One minute I'm walking down the street, and the next thing I know I'm in some guy's car on my way to help solve a kidnapping. It turns out maybe it wasn't so much a kidnapping. Then I'm running through the streets like a crazy person. Who even knows what those guys are up to?"

"Only you," he answered, still chuckling a bit before he pulled himself together. "Well, look, let's just get this done. We'll go find the house, we'll call the local cops, and we'll figure out what we're looking at. OK?"

She nodded in agreement, and they got up and walked out of Clint's office. He was standing not too far away from the door, waiting on them with an expectant expression on his face. She thought it was sweet; he was trying to look out for her.

"Are you OK?" Clint asked, anxiously noticing her red face and damp eyes.

"Totally fine." She smiled and gave him a huge hug. "Thank you so much for being here for me. I appreciate your help."

"Anytime, kid."

"And I'm sorry if I scared the new guy. He looked a little freaked out when I came in."

"Naw, Drew's a good dude. He's an industry vet."

"Huh," she answered. "Wonder why I don't know him? I thought I knew almost everybody in the industry in town."

"He's been around, worked as a tech for a couple of other local guys before he ended up here. This is his first sales gig though, so that's probably why you've never met."

"Sorry to interrupt," Will broke in, looking impatient. "But we need to get going."

CHAPTER NINE

FINDING SCOTT NICHOLS

GETTING into Will's car felt a little too familiar, and she slipped her seat belt on as he started the car, a little grin on his face, still kind of chuckling to himself.

"What? What's so funny?"

"Nothing. I just forgot that even in the middle of all of this nonsense, you have the wherewithal to stand there and have an arbitrary conversation with one of your customers. Always be closing, right?"

"It's not arbitrary, and he's not a customer anymore," she answered, slightly offended. "I was just being polite, and it's important. I have to know the people. I make my living now from referrals. Maybe that guy has got a job he's going to sell that he could use me on. I need the work, Will."

"I understand that," he said. "This is just like the time a guy was shooting a gun at you, and you took the time to grab your purse before you ran. We need to work on your survival skills."

"I'm not supposed to need survival skills. I'm in sales!" she exclaimed, and the look he gave her was so condescending. "Whatever, let's just get this done."

She gave him basic directions. They were a little random, but the best she could think of to get back to the house after explaining the route that she'd taken while running and using the butcher shop as a landmark. He nodded, looking at a map on his phone. She was impressed he'd gotten a smartphone since their breakup; he was so anti-technology. Once they had a fairly good idea of where the house was located, Will pulled out into traffic and headed out. They drove in silence for a little bit, both checking out the window and watching the houses go by. They had to loop around a few times as Cam got her bearings, because most of the streets were one-way. As they drove, Will's phone rang, and he answered it with a confused expression on his face. After listening to the caller for a minute, he handed her the phone.

"It's for you," he said.

She took the phone warily. Who would be calling her on Will's phone?

"Hello?" Oh wow, it was Bill. She'd forgotten to call him in the allotted time, and he'd done what she asked and called the police. And being Bill, he called the police officer he knew; he'd called Will. If it was a contest, she'd just kicked her brother's ass in terms of getting her police assistance.

She repeated her story for the third time and promised to

call him after they found the house. After assuring him she was OK and hanging up, she handed the phone back to Will. He took it again with a laugh.

"I'm glad to see I've been amusing you lately. What's so funny now?"

"I'm just laughing because between Clint, Bill, Phil, and all your other little work buddies, you have this whole crew of A/V nerds who want to come down to rescue you."

"Yeah," she answered dryly. "It's called having friends." There was something in his face at that answer that she didn't like. She didn't want to believe it, but maybe Will was lonely. Or maybe that was the reason he walked away from her and their burgeoning relationship. Maybe he didn't like that most of her friends were guys. Some men couldn't handle it. Regardless, he was stopped from answering when she exclaimed, "There! That's the house," pointing out the window at the distinctive brownstone.

They pulled over to the side of the road, and Will immediately got on his phone to call the local police department. He had a buddy who worked out of Brooklyn, and they said they'd be on their way shortly. Cameron made a move like she was going to get out of the car, and Will put his hand on her arm, stopping her.

"What? Aren't we going to check it out?"

"No, we're not going to check it out. I think we're going to do the smart thing and wait for backup this time. It looks like it's abandoned now, but what if we rush in there to a crowd of what you said were, you know, eight armed mercenaries. The right thing to do is wait for backup. Not rush blindly in."

She rolled her eyes, but they waited, traffic streaming around them, in the kind of awkward silence you can only share with someone you used to date. She felt slightly chastised at his words, but it was hard to argue when she knew he was right. She did tend to be a bit impulsive.

When the first unmarked police car pulled up behind them, Will motioned for her to stay and got out to talk to the detective who came out of the first car. He pointed to the house and then he pointed to her. It seemed like he was effusively telling her story, and she could just imagine what he was saying.

"Oh, you see, my idiot sort-of ex-girlfriend got in a car with a bunch of random dudes with guns, ended up at this house, which they told her belonged to a kidnapping victim, and she innocently downloaded their entire electronic systems use history for them before realizing that they were probably criminals. Yeah, she's not that bright, but she sure is cute."

Grr, she thought she might have just been projecting, but the whole day was turning into one big, stressful mess. She wanted to get out of the car. She wanted to hear what they were talking about. It was unnerving, being left out of the conversation and the investigation. She saw more cop cars pull up. Some marked patrol cars this time with uniformed officers getting out, joining their huddle before taking up sentry positions around the perimeter. She saw different members of the group break off and go to walk around the exterior of the house. She watched the detective walk up and knock on the front door. As she watched them look in the windows, she was more convinced than ever that no one was there. Jack and his team must have left right after they discovered her missing. After a few more moments of talking with the detective, Will finally walked back to the car, and it looked like she might get some answers after all.

He got back in the driver's seat and started to put his seat belt back on.

"What are you doing?" asked Cameron. "Aren't we going in there?"

"No," he answered, starting up the car. "I'm taking you home."

"What do you mean?" she asked. "Don't I have to give them a statement? Aren't they even going to go inside and look around?"

"Yes," he said. "But the investigation is in their hands now. It's not my jurisdiction. I've given them your preliminary statement. They'll be calling you to come in and give an official one soon. They need to get permission from the homeowner to enter, as there is no immediate threat. And there's no visible evidence of a crime."

"No evidence of a crime? I was kidnapped in that house!"

"No, you weren't. You willingly went into someone's home. I won't say you broke in, but it's pretty damn close. Also, you should stop saying that word. You're going to turn into the girl who cried kidnap, and then no one will believe you next time."

Next time? Like hell, she was getting herself into one of these situations again. She bit back the emotions she was feeling and tried to approach Will in a calm manner. "You said someone's home. Does that mean it's not Scott Nichols's home?"

"Nope. That house isn't registered to Scott Nichols. It belongs to a corporation. The police are going to track them down and find out if anyone's been living there. They also found Scott Nichols. Scott and his family are all alive and well, and very confused. They don't even live in New York. They live in Atlanta; he works for the CDC."

Well, that made sense, she thought. Being in virology, the CDC was probably the perfect place for a guy like Scott Nichols, but that still didn't explain anything. The real question was who were Jack and his team looking for, and had she helped, or had she hurt?

CHAPTER TEN

DISAPPOINTMENT

"SO that's it?" she asked as Will pulled out into traffic, heading back toward the city. "I get abducted, and we just leave and somebody else is going to solve the crime. You're not even going to look into it?"

"There's nothing for me to look into. Those guys are probably long gone by now, and until they figure out whose house it is, they're not going to know what they're looking for. The police are going to go in, look for evidence, lift some prints to see what they can find. That's all they can do at this point. Without more information, there's nothing to do. What do you want me to do, Cameron? Where should I go? Who should I be looking for?"

"I gave you his picture; can you at least put an alert out or something?"

"Of course, I passed it along to the detective in charge

and he'll issue a BOLO. But again, they'll need more information before they can move forward."

She guessed it was understandable, but it still pissed her off. He was acting like what happened didn't even matter. She'd been terrified earlier that day, and what would have happened if she hadn't been able to get away from Jack and his team? And for Will to act like it was no big deal, it just hurt. She couldn't understand it.

He reached over and put his hand on her knee, which jolted her a little bit. "It'll be OK, Cameron. I'm going to follow up. The detective on the case is a friend of mine, and he's going to keep me posted. I'll keep you in the loop as soon as they have something to go on, and I'll let you know what it is."

"OK." It was reasonable, but still, she wasn't liking the way this was going. She didn't like it when Will left her out, and that also had maybe been a contributing factor as to why their relationship failed. They weren't on the same team anymore. She wasn't a detective. She wasn't privy to his investigations, and for somebody who liked solving puzzles, being left out was hard to handle.

"Maybe in the meantime, you could help me out with something else," he asked.

It was like he was reading her mind, she thought, her ears perking up. "Help you with what?" she asked.

"It's a new case I'm working on, and there's an element of electronics to it. We haven't been satisfied with the answers we've been getting."

"OK," she said, intrigued. "Tell me about it."

"It's a series of arsons," he said. Again, reaching toward her. This time not to touch her but to reach for the seat behind her and bring up a folder. He laid it on her lap. It was a huge folder, thick, with lots of little subfolders in there with tabs and colored sticky notes. "There's been a series of arsons. The point of origin was the equipment rooms at several high-net-worth individuals' houses. There's no sign of a break-in, and they weren't considered high-profile crimes until this last one. Someone finally died, so now it's upgraded from arson to murder."

"Why would you say there's an element of electronics in it?"

"All of the victims have smart-home systems, and the fires started around the electronics. They're all different systems, and there's no one component that's present in all of the projects. We can't tell whether the fires were started by certain components, or if the location of the fires is completely coincidental. Maybe it's just where the arsonist liked to set them. We don't know."

She began to leaf through the paperwork as they became immersed in stopped traffic trying to get to the bridge. Trying to be efficient, she skimmed the first page summaries at the beginning of each of the divided sections separated by tabs. She was just starting to put some thoughts together when she saw Will pull out his phone and dial a number. He kept the phone in his lap and kept pressing buttons.

"What the hell are you doing?" she asked, bewildered.

"I'm checking my voicemail."

"Huh?" she asked, still not getting it.

"I'm calling my voicemail to get my messages," he repeated.

"You're calling your voicemail?"

"Yes."

"To get the messages on your cell phone, not from a messaging service or something?"

"Yes."

That was it. She cracked up laughing, glancing between Will and his phone.

"What's so funny?"

Cameron reached over and took the iPhone from him and ended the call. She glanced at the road; traffic still wasn't moving. She held the phone up so he could see it.

"See this little button that looks like a tape recorder?" He nodded in answer. She hit the button and a long list of names and numbers popped up. "This is your voicemail." She hit the top name on the list and held the phone in his view again. "See this? You have visual voicemail. It shows you the text of your messages. You can read them, or you can hit that little play icon and listen to the message. You can also call back from there. You don't have to call anybody to get your messages."

"Huh." He appeared thoughtful as he took the phone back from her and messed with the application.

"You may want to delete some of those. Your voicemail may be full, and people might not be able to leave new messages."

He just grunted in acknowledgment and kept playing with the phone. She didn't know why his ineptitude with technology was so endearing when, with most people, having to explain something so simple would have pissed her off. But it was. He was like a kid with a new toy.

"Why'd you even get that phone? You hate technology," she asked with a small smile as she watched him fumble with the device.

"I don't hate technology." He gave her a sharp look like he was offended, but he acquiesced quickly at her unconvinced expression. "OK, OK, we were required to get them at work. They took away our access badges and put it all on our phones. I had to get one or I'd never be able to get in my office again."

She shook her head, grinning at him, and turned her attention back to the report.

"Were they all different A/V integrators that worked on the projects?" she asked as she leafed through the pages.

"A/V integrators?" he asked, not familiar with the reference.

"Yeah, it's what we sometimes call our dealers. You know, my customers when I worked at SmartTech."

"Gotcha, then yes," he answered, putting his phone away as traffic started to move again. "All different companies, all different components, obviously there's some overlap, but again nothing that holds true for all the fires."

"Maybe it's just a guy who really hates A/V."

"Maybe," Will replied, but he sounded doubtful.

She gave a cursory glance to the page she was on and saw handwritten notes from someone about all the electronics. She knew immediately that Will had been talking to somebody else in her industry. She was disappointed that even with the difficulties between them, he didn't come to her first. Was their relationship so far gone he felt like he had to seek out help from somebody else? That he couldn't come to her if he needed her? That hurt a little. He was the first person she had thought of today when she needed help. She wished it were the same for him.

"Who do you talk to about this?" she asked. "I can see that you've been working with somebody else in the industry." She tried to keep the bitterness out of her voice, but she didn't think she was successful if Will's expression was anything to go by. He looked hesitant, as if he was carefully selecting his words so he wouldn't upset her.

"I asked your friend Phil for help. He got us some assistance from SmartTech."

She was stunned, and her face got hot. She tried to hold perfectly still and not show her reaction, but inside she was fuming. That. Little. Traitor.

Phil Vance was one of Cameron's best friends and her former coworker at SmartTech. She could not believe Phil would work with Will and not even tell her. They still had their Friday afternoon calls, even though she wasn't with the team at SmartTech anymore. She talked to him all the time. Almost every day. They were still close, and he hadn't told her anything about it. How could he hide something like this from her?

And moreover, how could Will go to SmartTech? After they'd fired her? There were so many other companies in her industry he could have reached out to. To go to her old employer felt like a slap in the face.

"I told him not to tell you, Cameron." Again, it was like he was reading her mind; was she that transparent? "Don't be mad at Phil. He couldn't tell you."

She chose not to answer and instead distract herself so she didn't explode. Cameron dug a little deeper into the files to get a little better idea of the case as they pulled off the bridge headed back into Manhattan. There were different files labeled with the names of the victims, and as she read through, a sneaky suspicion started settling in her gut, and she thought she might have the answer as to why Will hadn't come to her first.

"These are all the names of Synergistic board members," she said flatly. Wait, she thought, spotting another name in the file. "And Steve? They went after Steve too?" Steve Perkins was her former boss and had fired her from SmartTech. Awkward was a tame word for their relationship these days; it hadn't quite reached openly hostile, but it was damn close. At least that explained why Will had gone to SmartTech. They were already involved.

"Yes. Every victim was on the board at Synergistic, plus Steve."

Jesus. Would her life ever be free of Synergistic? In the past few months, she'd had a lot of regrets about how she'd handled the incident with the HomeTech Hubs and Matt Rodriguez's murder. Her actions had cost her a job she loved, and worse, a friend. She thought it was all behind her, but it looked like Synergistic wasn't done with her yet. If she could go back and change it all, she wondered if she would've just left that chip where she found it. If she had never investigated the anomaly in the popular consumer electronics device, her life would've been a whole lot simpler. Casey would still have been alive, and she'd still have had a job. And she never would've gotten in some random guy's car, no matter how good the money was.

"You didn't ask me for help because you thought I'd done this," she said with a sigh. Resigned to the fact that whatever she felt or had felt for Will, he obviously didn't see her the same way. Not if he could ever see her as a suspect. Her last bit of hope for a relationship between them died. She'd never really felt like it was completely over before. There had always seemed to be a possibility of them reconnecting again when the timing was better. Not anymore, not if he believed she could be capable of murder.

"No," he said emphatically, glancing over, trying to meet her eyes and watch the road at the same time. "I would never think that you would do anything like this."

"You went behind my back. You went to one of my best friends and asked him for help. You told him not to tell me about it, but you don't think I had anything to do with it?" She didn't take her eyes off the street in front of her; she couldn't even look at him. She didn't believe him for a second. Actions always spoke louder than words.

"No, Cameron. I never thought you were capable of this. But there was some discussion at the office, and we thought it was best to leave you out of it until we had more information. You lost a lot because of Synergistic. We just needed to make sure we didn't create a situation that could've made going to trial a challenge. Muddy the evidence or whatnot."

In her mind that was the same thing as being a suspect. "Was it Kim's idea to keep me out?" Kim Goodrich, the Assistant District Attorney, had never liked Cam. And she didn't bother to keep her feelings hidden.

"No, it never got that far. It was Gil's decision."

So, Will's boss, Captain Gil Lovett, kept her out. That was interesting. She always thought he liked her. "What changed?" she asked.

"Nothing really. But after the last fire and the death of one of the executives' children, we knew we needed all the resources we could get. We have no real leads, and we're not getting any closer. I got Captain Lovett to agree to let you look at the case."

"Let me get this straight," she said. "I'm kidnapped off the street today, and you can't be bothered to look into that; you just pass it off to someone else. But you expect me to drop everything to investigate your arson-slash-murder case? Sorry, Will, if you're not interested in helping me, I'm not interested in helping you."

They were getting close to her building, and she was almost bouncing in her seat with adrenaline. She couldn't wait to be out of the car and away from Will. How could he think she would do something like set fire to people's houses? Murder someone? A child? Over what? A job?

She wasn't mad at Synergistic. She wasn't even mad at Steve for firing her. She didn't blame them for her situation. She blamed herself for that. She fully owned the choices that led her to her present situation. She may not like it, but she wasn't pawning the responsibility off on anybody else. She'd made mistakes; she'd own them.

What would the point be to hurt the board members? They hadn't done anything to her. The three conspirators who planned to use the company's HomeTech Hub to spy on people were the ones she had a problem with. And they had all been arrested and were in prison. She'd helped put them there. She didn't have any animosity toward anyone else at the company. In fact, she felt kind of sorry for them. Having to deal with the fallout from their principals' criminal acts had caused the company's stock to tank. They had to sell off most of their assets, fire most of their employees, and they were back to only selling computer components. And not very good ones, or at least not as innovative as what they used to produce. They even lost their cool office in Manhattan. She couldn't imagine what it was like to be on the board of Synergistic right then; they were a shell of what they once were. No one should have any reason to hurt them. They had hurt themselves plenty.

Will sighed as he pulled into the loading zone in front of her apartment building, snapping her out of her thoughts. "Just take the file. Just look at it; there's a full equipment list from every fire. If there's anything you need to know about the cases you can't find in there, call me. Check it out, and let us know if you find anything we should take a closer look at. We'll pay you for your time."

She shook her head. "It's nice to know what you think about me. First, I'm an arsonist, then I'm a killer, and now

I'm a whore who will do anything for a paycheck." He pulled back from her, his face betraying his shock at her words.

She wanted to scream. She wanted to freak out, throw a tantrum, and just rage at Will. She'd thought they had had something together. She certainly had a lot of respect for him. How he could think so little of her after what they'd shared. Something inside her cracked. She was furious, and she could tell he noticed as he was staring at her hands. She was gripping those files way too tightly; the whites of her knuckles were showing. She choked the feeling of betrayal back, sucked the emotion down, and calmed herself. It wouldn't do any good to throw a fit. It wasn't the kind of thing a person like Will responded to; he was much too reserved, and sometimes silence spoke louder than anything else.

She didn't even glance back at him as she opened the car door. She simply threw the file onto the floorboard, unclipped her seat belt, and got out of the car. Without another word, she walked calmly toward her building. As far as Cameron was concerned, there wasn't anything left to say.

CHAPTER ELEVEN

NEW CAM

NEVER let them see you squirm. She kept repeating the mantra in her head as she walked toward her building, but she was so mad she wanted to scream. Or better yet, punch something. No matter what he said, she knew, she just knew that he'd at least for a moment considered that she was capable of killing someone. She glanced in the bodega window and saw the cigarette display over Eytan's head as he was checking someone out at the register, and it took even more effort and supreme mental conditioning to keep walking. She'd quit smoking again, finally, and she wasn't going to give in to weakness and pick it up again just because Will upset her. She was stronger than that.

Walking into her apartment, she shut and locked the door, then immediately pressed her back to it. Shutting her eyes and dropping her bag, she took a long exhale. How could things have gone so wrong? The day started off well enough. She'd met with a much-needed new client and closed a new deal. It was a beautiful day; she was going to go to the farmers' market. And then... disaster. OK, she thought, opening her eyes and taking a deep breath. Time to get moving. She still had work to do on top of all the crap that had been dumped into her lap. No time to relax. She needed to act.

The next step was completing her coming home routine. Bra off, contacts out, glasses and yoga pants on. Pouring a bourbon and retrieving her bag from where she'd dumped it by the door, she cracked her laptop open. Best to get the final contract for her new client finished before anything else. That way she could focus. Then, if Will wasn't going to find out who Jack was and what he'd gotten her into, she was.

Twenty minutes later, she closed her computer with a powerful thud. Job done. It wasn't her best work, but it was all she could manage at the moment. She said a silent prayer to the A/V gods that the clients signed the paperwork and sent the deposit quickly, because she desperately needed the cash, and she didn't see Jack sending her that ten grand he promised after her dramatic exit. She glanced at her watch. It was only seven thirty. Damn, it felt so much later than that.

Rubbing her face with her hands, she prepared for the next task of the day. Pulling up her video conferencing app, she dialed Bill. Cam turned on her seventy-five-inch LED TV and threw the call onto the screen, waiting for him to answer.

"Jesus Christ, what took you so long?" he exclaimed, looking haggard. "What the hell happened today?"

"Can we just not for a second?" she asked, taking a sip of her Maker's and Diet Coke. "I just need a few minutes to chill before I tell the story again. How was your day?"

He blinked at her for a few moments before deciding how to answer. He must have noticed she was at her limit, because he backed off his inquisition and gave her a much-needed distraction. "We're back-ordered three months on touchscreens."

"What?" she asked. That came out of left field.

"I said, we're back-ordered three months on touchscreens."

"No, I heard you. I just don't understand. How do you sell a home automation system without the touchscreens?"

"Lots and lots of iPads," he answered dryly and with an eye roll. "I've learned way more than I ever wanted to know about global supply chain logistics today."

"Oh, really? What did you learn? Other than the phrase 'global supply chain logistics.'"

"It boils down to two things. Either the global supply chain for semiconductors is literally the most complex and intricate system ever designed in the history of mankind, or our logistics guy screwed up real bad and is trying to hide his mistake in a complex web of lies and really big words."

Cameron laughed. His answer was the kind of quick-witted retort she'd come to expect from Bill. His joke still caught her a little off guard, and some of her drink escaped her mouth. She reached for a napkin to catch the liquid dribbling down her chin and asked, "So, which is it?"

"Eh, a little bit of both, I think. Regardless, my life is fucked for the next few months. You know all the dealers are going to get pissed. If we don't have touchscreens, they can't finish their jobs, which means they can't get paid. It's gonna be a shitshow."

"Glad I don't have to deal with it," she said with a smirk, toasting him with her drink.

"Yeah, it's going to be interesting to see how the new guy handles it."

Ah, the new guy. Her replacement. It stung a bit when the guys told her that her position at SmartTech had been filled. It was stupid. Everyone was replaceable. She knew that. They had to have somebody to do the job. His name was Harris Brown. He came from a really big consumer-facing speaker company that was a household name but basically made junk. He'd never done B2B, or business-to-business sales before. His only experience in sales was selling to end users. Cameron knew him a bit, in that she'd seen him around at industry events. She'd always thought he was kind of an idiot and exceedingly dull. Neither were good qualities in salespeople. She couldn't believe Steve had hired him.

"How's he doing?" she asked neutrally. She didn't want to put her bias or hurt feelings on Bill, but God, she resented him. He was in her job. Going to her meetings. With her customers. It had been months, and she still hadn't gotten used to it.

"New Cam is an idiot."

"Seriously?" She didn't want to admit it to herself, but that did make her a little happy. For the first time that day, it felt like someone was on her side. Even if it was petty.

"Well, he doesn't have much of a sense of humor. He doesn't like it when we call him New Cam to his face, and he has no idea what he's doing. But what do I care? As long as he stays away from my territory, it doesn't bother me. Enough of this; what the hell happened to you today?"

She blew out a long breath and laid it out for him.

"To summarize," he said after she'd finished. "You blundered into some sort of criminal activity that you then actively participated in and told Will to suck it when he asked you for help because you got your feelings hurt. How do you get yourself into these things? It's like being friends with 'Scooby-freakin'-Doo."

"Ruh-roh."

"Not funny."

"I know. But just to clarify, I extricated myself from the situation when I noticed it was shady. I then called the cops instead of trying to investigate on my own, and then I declined to get involved with the police in another caper. Regardless of how I got there, I think that's growth."

"Agreed, but you did still get into an armed stranger's car. So don't go patting yourself on the back too much. And so, the question remains, what are you going to do now?"

"Well, since Will isn't taking this Jack character seriously, I'm going to look into that a bit. I don't want anything there to come back and bite me in the ass. But before that, the first thing I'm going to do is ask Phil what the hell he's been up to."

"Call him now," Bill said, his eyes lighting up. He always did like to be in the middle of the shit.

"OK, stand by. I'll conference him in."

CHAPTER TWELVE

TEAM MEETING

"HEY, guys!" Phil answered, excitement evident on his face as he popped up on her screen next to Bill. "Glad you're both here. Cam, I need you to update the spreadsheet."

"What happened?" she asked automatically. Temporarily sidetracked from her mission to confront him for keeping secrets at Will's request. "You got kicked out of a 'dealer's office today?"

The group used to keep an online Google doc of all Bill's dates. After his divorce, he dated so often and so many different women, it became impossible to keep them straight. To avoid unnecessary confusion, they'd kept a shared online document listing all his dates' names. But recently Bill had settled down and gotten a girlfriend. So, the spreadsheet had adapted. They deleted all the old info, and it was no longer used to track Bill's women. Instead, they used it to keep track of when a dealer kicked one of the reps out of their offices during a meeting. That Phil would want to add to it was shocking. Bill was the king of getting asked to leave meetings; it happened to him all the time. Cameron was next in the tally, having been asked to leave a few times, but it never happened to Phil. He was far too polite and way too even-tempered.

"Yep," he answered proudly. "I got kicked out of Michael's office today." Another anomaly: Michael was Phil's biggest customer, and they were great friends.

"What'd you do?" asked Bill, completely focused on the screen. He was thoroughly invested in the story.

"Nothing, really; he completely overreacted. I was trying to chat with him about starting the plan for putting together a big end-of-year order to max out his rebate, and he just lost it. In retrospect, it probably wasn't the best time to bring it up as he did just give me a two-hundred-thousand-dollar order last week and had just finished telling me about a client he couldn't get the final payment from, but still. His reaction was way over-the-top. Even for him." Phil was chuckling to himself but stopped when he noticed they weren't laughing with him. "What's up with you guys? Cam, why are you so quiet?"

"I saw Will Justus today." She switched back to the real reason for the call, taking a sip of her drink to steady her nerves. "Is there anything at all you've been meaning to tell me?"

"Don't freak out," he said, putting his hands up in a placating manner, attempting to calm her. His voice took on an unnaturally soothing tone, as if he was saying "nice doggy" and praying she wouldn't attack him. "It isn't that big of a deal. He asked me to look at several lists of equipment to see if I saw any connections. I didn't see anything, so I got him in contact with Steve. That's it. They asked me not to tell anyone. Specifically, not to tell you. It was just a few hours. If it was anything more than that, I would've told you."

"You didn't think it was weird they asked you for help?" Cameron asked.

"No, why would I?"

"They thought I was a suspect!" Cameron exclaimed. "They thought I was the arsonist! That's why they asked you and not me."

"What arson?" Phil asked, looking bewildered.

"The fires set in the houses with the equipment rooms you looked at, you idiot. Didn't they tell you about that?"

"No, they didn't tell me anything about it. They only asked if I saw a pattern in the equipment or could tie it back to any one particular dealer."

"And could you?" asked Bill, ignoring the personal drama.

"No, they were all pretty standard equipment lists. A lot of generic gear you could get from anywhere, but they were all well-designed. Not all of them were SmartTech systems. I didn't see anything special in them, and they didn't tell me why they were asking. I'm so sorry, Cameron. If I'd have known they were looking at you for anything, I'd have told you. Honestly. It was weeks ago and very brief. It just didn't seem important. Plus, you know, you broke up with him, so…."

"I did not break up with him! He ghosted me! Are you serious right now? Did he tell you I broke up with him?"

Bill jumped in before Phil had a chance to reply, trying to steer the conversation back on track. "If you connected him with Steve, then he must have gotten one of the tech-support guys to check it out too. Had to be one of the Mikes."

"But which Mike?" Cameron wondered, still smarting a bit about Phil's comment. "Smart Mike, Stupid Mike, or Mike that's sleeping with the girl in customer service?"

"Stupid Mike is the one who's sleeping with the girl in customer service," said Phil.

"Oh," Cam answered. "I thought there were three Mikes."

"There are," said Phil. "The third Mike is Marketing Mike."

"It has to be Smart Mike," Bill broke in. "His lips are always firmly attached to Steve's ass. He's his go-to in tech support these days."

Damn it. That was no help to her. Smart Mike was the complete opposite of Casey. He was the worst. Super arrogant and always confrontational with the sales team; he wasn't one of her favorite people. Cameron had never had a good relationship with him. She couldn't imagine him giving her the time of day after the way she had left the company.

"Well, that's no help. He'll never talk to me. And I'm sorry I got upset, Phil. I'm not mad at you," she said.

Realizing it was true. It wasn't fair for her to take her anger at Will out on Phil. "I'm just disappointed in the way things turned out with Will. He says he didn't consider me a suspect, but on some level, he must have. Otherwise, he would've come to me."

"Why were you considered a suspect? What was the crime? They didn't tell me anything. I even asked them to show me pictures of the equipment racks. I thought I could learn something from the wiring, but no dice. They said it was part of an ongoing investigation."

"Okay, one more time so we're all on the same page. Someone set fires in some of the Synergistic board members' houses and in Steve's house. In the last fire, one of the 'executives' sons died. He was only eleven. That's why Will is on the case now. All the fires were started in the equipment rooms. That's why they asked you about them. Everybody got it now?"

Phil was nodding along, thoughtful. "Steve's house too? Wow, I haven't heard anything around the office about it."

Bill chimed in. "No offense, Cam. I know you didn't do it, but you have to see why they'd be looking at you. I mean who else would have a beef with Synergistic? They're pretty much in the shitter now."

"There could be a million reasons. Maybe it's because their business tanked. Maybe it was a shareholder who lost a ton of money. Maybe it was a former employee who's pissed they got fired, and this is their way of going postal. Maybe they all belong to some freaky sex cult. Who knows?" Cam responded, rolling her eyes at Bill's insinuation that she had a motive. "I'm more concerned with how they did it. I got a brief look at the case files in Will's car today. They couldn't find evidence of any break-ins or any incendiary devices. And I know components can sometimes get pretty hot, but hot enough to cause a fire? And how could you even control that?"

"I know you were trying to make a point, but it would've been better if you'd taken Will's files instead of storming off in a huff," Bill commented.

She flicked him off in the monitor. He smirked. "We don't need the files. We have something better than that. We have our combined technical knowledge and Phil's memory."

"That doesn't sound like much," Bill replied skeptically.

"Sure, it is, but forget the details for a minute. Hypothetically, if you were going to use electronics to set a fire, how would you do it?"

"I don't know," Bill answered, his brow furrowed in thought. He was the most technical of all of them. If any of them could figure it out, Cam was betting on him. "Cable boxes and amps get the hottest, but anything like that has a fail-safe built in, so they either shut off or kick on a fan."

"Plus, all of the system lists I saw were well designed," Phil added. "They all had ventilation and fans built in. I don't think you could count on stuff just getting hot."

"Is it possible to remove the fail-safes? Or disable the fans?" she asked.

"Probably," Bill answered. "But again, you'd lose a lot of control. You couldn't be sure if they'd be used enough to create the kind of heat necessary to cause a fire or if they'd just burn themselves out. And you'd for sure never be able to predict when it would happen. I see two issues with that scenario. First, you'd have to physically do it. And you said there'd been no signs of a break-in. So how could they tamper with the equipment? Second, the timing. You said, until the last fire, the houses were empty and no one had been killed. You have to assume that was by design. There's no way to control the result if you went about it that way. They had to have done something else. Something remotely, most likely."

Something about that nagged in Cameron's brain… remotely. Oh shit, she knew how they did it.

"I got it," she said. "Phil, were there aftermarket routers installed on all the jobs?"

"I think so. But so what? Those would never get hot enough to cause a fire."

"You think they used EvryWare, don't you?" Bill answered, catching on to her line of thought.

EvryWare was a relatively new remote-management system almost every integrator used on all their projects. It allowed dealers to connect with their 'clients' systems from anywhere. It gave dealers the ability to troubleshoot problems without having to go on-site. It had been a major improvement in customer service and tech support in her industry. No longer did dealers have to spend the time and expense of a trip to a customer's house just to reboot an outlet or update the firmware. EvryWare allowed them to do it from their phones while standing in line at a

Starbucks. It would also explain why none of the equipment was the same across all the arson sites. EvryWare was built into most of the routers her customers used from all the major brands. It was also sold as a separate appliance so it could be installed on any jobsite. Once connected to a network, you could have control over anything in the house from anywhere in the world. As long as you had an internet connection.

"Exactly," Cam answered. "Phil, think. Could every site have had EvryWare installed in it?"

"Oh yeah, I bet they did," he agreed, nodding. "I'm such a dumbass for not putting it together."

"No, you're not. It's so standard these days, it wouldn't have stood out. But that still doesn't explain how you could use that to start a fire," Cameron replied.

"I bet I know how they did it," Bill said. "Firmware updates."

"What?" asked Cam, not seeing how firmware updates could be the cause. All electronics were constantly getting firmware updates, and they never resulted in fires.

"You'd have to use an amp of something that gets extremely hot. But if you wrote a program for a firmware update that took an insanely long amount of time, you could catch one on fire, and then everything else would go up. Think about it. Fail-safes don't kick in during a firmware update. Electronics are taught not to shut off when updates are running so you don't brick the component. If you wrote your own program, sufficiently overworked the system, and let it run long enough. Boom. Fire. And you could do it from anywhere."

"Holy shit," Phil said softly.

"Ditto," said Cam. "Theoretically, it could be done. And it really wouldn't be that hard. But if that's what they did, it should be easy to track. To use EvryWare, you have to work for the integrator who did the install to get access. You have to have a username and password, and there would be a record of who initialized the update. We can track who did it."

"Maybe," Bill said, "maybe not. Anybody that's worked for an integrator would have the knowledge to set up a bogus account with a fake username. And EvryWare wouldn't be able to track that. They're huge now. They must register tons of new accounts every day."

"Agreed, but at least it's a place to start. I'll let Will know," she said with resignation.

"You sure? I can call him if you'd rather not," Phil offered.

"No, it's okay. I want to get an update on what the Brooklyn police learned about today anyway. And it won't do any good to avoid him. Better to just face it. Plus, I need to apologize."

"Apologize?" asked Phil skeptically. "You?"

"Yeah, I overreacted today. I think I let the stress of everything get to me. Will didn't do anything wrong. I shouldn't have taken my frustration out on him."

"Look at you, being all mature about it," joked Bill.

"Whatever," she answered. "Look, I'm going to let you guys go. I need to grab something to eat and head to bed.

But I'll update the spreadsheet tonight. I wouldn't want Phil's moment of glory to go unrecorded. Later, guys."

Cam closed out the call, and her TV screen went blank. The shiny dark glass reflected tiny sparkles of light that filtered through her window. She needed to get up and throw together something for dinner, but instead, she stretched out on her couch tucking a throw pillow under her head. A new bright-red sofa to replace the one that had gotten destroyed by the HomeTech Hub killer when she'd sent someone to break into her apartment and trash it. She hadn't quite broken it in yet, and it wasn't as comfortable as the last one. Or maybe it was just revisionist history, her remembering everything from before as better than it actually was.

It would be a huge bombshell to the industry if someone was using EvryWare to cause fires. Why would anyone do that? Who would take an amazing piece of technology and turn it into something so sinister? It just went to show that human ingenuity could be used to create miracles as well as tragedies. Technology doesn't have morality. Only people do. This was really going to frustrate the police. How did you even begin to track a killer that didn't even go to the crime scene?

With a sigh, she got up off the couch and made her way into the kitchen. Looked like ramen noodles again. Jesus, she had to get the deposit from the deal she closed. Her life was coming dangerously close to resembling that of a college student.

An hour and an unsatisfying meal later, she settled into her bed for the night. She arranged all the pillows around herself, creating a little nest she could snuggle into. She should call her brother. It was the right thing to do. She had scared him today, and regardless of how strained their relationship was, he'd come through for her. Christian wasn't a bad guy, but he was five years older than Cameron and that meant they hadn't spent a lot of time together as children. Add to that the fact that they were both highly competitive and stubborn, and you had a recipe for friction every time they got together. She blamed a lot of the strain in their relationship on their parents. Both Cricket and Rush Caldwell were high-achieving and expected the same from their children. They nurtured a highly competitive home environment in which Cameron had always felt like she never quite measured up to her brother.

She glanced at the clock; it was almost eleven, which meant eight on the West Coast. His family would be in the middle of dinner. The West Coast Caldwell clan sat down for dinner at precisely seven thirty every weekday night. She shuddered to think how pretentious those meals must be. She certainly couldn't interrupt family dinner; that would just be rude. Grateful for the excuse not to have to deal with Christian again, she grabbed her phone to text Will.

I think I know how the arsonist set the fires. Call me tomorrow.

She set the phone on her nightstand and rolled over to get comfy. But before she could fall asleep, her phone beeped. Looked like Will had texted her back. Cam was slightly surprised he knew how to text after the voicemail debacle. But when she looked at her screen, it wasn't a text message, it was a notification from her bank. Confused, she sat up and opened her banking app. Logging in to check, she saw the notice was for a deposit. Clicking into her account, she saw it. Holy shit, there was a deposit for nine thousand nine hundred and ninety-nine dollars.

Jack had paid her. And he paid her just under the ten thousand dollars he'd promised to make sure she wouldn't be taxed on it. Considerate, but it confused her. On one hand, she was grateful. She really needed the money. On the other hand, did this make her a criminal? She thought it over for a few minutes, but unable to come to a conclusion, she decided to tackle that moral dilemma later. Shrugging it off, she fluffed her pillow, rolled over, and fell asleep.

CHAPTER THIRTEEN

FANTASIES OF BACON, EGG, AND CHEESE

WAKING up Tuesday morning, Cameron groaned. It was seven o'clock and, in her opinion way too early to be awake. It was one of life's great mysteries that she could sleep all day when she had to be up for something, but when she had the luxury of staying in bed all day, she was up at the crack of dawn. She rolled over and checked her phone; no response from Will.

She got up and shuffled into the bathroom. She did the bare minimum to make herself presentable. Brushing her teeth and pulling her hair up into a ponytail. She didn't have to like being up so early, but she could at least be well fed. She grabbed a hoodie off the floor, her glasses off her nightstand, and jammed her feet into some flip-flops she had left by the door. She fantasized about getting a bacon, egg, and cheese sandwich and a latte her whole ride down in the elevator.

Walking out the glass doors, Cameron looked up and stopped dead in her tracks. Will was leaning on his car, parked right in front of her building. Hip cocked on the front quarter panel, ankles crossed, he adopted a casual pose with a familiar paper bag in one hand and what she assumed was a latte in the other. Ugh, why was it your exes only showed up when you looked like shit? Or when you'd done something stupid like bumble into criminal activity and inadvertently assist in some kind of mischief? She couldn't catch a break. Slowly she made her way over to him, trying to decide how she was going to handle this. Showing up with breakfast took some effort. It was a nice gesture, and she had forgiven Phil. She could forgive Will too.

"Been waiting long?" she asked, taking the coffee from him when he offered it to her. She took a sip; she was right. It was a vanilla latte. She was so predictable.

"Not too long, but I was in for the duration. Knowing you, I could've been waiting here until noon."

"True. Guess you got lucky this morning. Too much on my mind, I couldn't go back to sleep."

"You figured it out?"

"I think so. I had a call last night with Bill and Phil, and we think we worked out how it was done. At least a strong possibility."

He nodded, thoughtfully, gazing at nothing. Then he looked down at her outfit. "Do you want to get dressed? Come down to the station and explain to the team?"

"Something wrong with the way I'm dressed?" she

teased, a mock-puzzled look on her face as she pulled out the hem of her hoodie, looking at it, then back at Will. Of course, there was; she didn't even have on a bra.

"I don't mind, but I thought you'd feel more comfortable in some real clothes."

She agreed, flip-flops were not ideal footwear for what she had in mind. "I'll change, but you go on ahead, and I'll meet you there. I'm going to get a shower, and I've got to make a stop first."

"Don't forget your sandwich," he said, handing her the bag. "Bacon, egg, and cheese. Your usual."

She took it from him and began to head back up to her place. Her usual. She was the same. Always the same. Will got a new partner, they'd replaced her at work, even permanent-bachelor Bill had a steady girlfriend now. Everything was changing except for her. Suddenly melancholy, she felt like everyone else was passing her by.

CHAPTER FOURTEEN

MANUAL LABOR

"WHAT about cables?" Drew asked, anxiously peering into the back of her Jeep at the mess of boxes they'd loaded in. "Do you have enough cables? I'm going to get you some more patch cables."

Cameron shook her head as she watched him scurry back into the shop from the warehouse she was parked in. He sure was a skittish little guy.

After seeing Will, she'd returned to her apartment and eaten her breakfast and gotten properly ready for the day. She'd showered and put on a decent outfit of jeans and a nice shirt, not going so far as to put on one of her old SmartTech suits. She didn't feel the need to dress up to impress the police. It had occurred to her that if she was going to convince anyone of her theory about being able to start the fires remotely, she was going to have to prove it was possible. It wasn't the kind of thing that nontechnical people could imagine. It was a common issue in her line of work. People had weird expectations about technology, and anything they didn't understand was placed strictly in the realm of science fiction. In general, they had no idea how technology worked. Most people used a fraction of the features on their most common electronics, like their cell phone or computer. Asking people with limited experience to understand that the components in stereo equipment could be used to start a fire was going to be exceptionally challenging. She'd need a demonstration if she wanted anyone to believe her.

Clint was again her lifesaver. When she'd called to ask him for some gear for her little experiment, he hadn't hesitated. He just told her to head to the office, that he wasn't in, but Drew would hook her up with anything she needed. Very generous for someone she'd told she wanted to set his stock on fire. She did have to promise Clint that the police would reimburse him for any equipment that was damaged. Even so, she was still going to owe him a nice bottle of wine when all this was over.

She was finally done playing a life-sized version of Tetris, trying to manipulate the big cardboard boxes filled with audio, networking, and infrastructure products into her Jeep, and she slammed the back shut in frustration. She moved around to the front and sat in the driver's seat, her feet hanging out the open door while she perused the equipment list. She checked everything off, confident she had all the parts she needed. Setting the list back on the passenger seat, she drummed her fingers on the steering wheel while she waited; even if she didn't need the cables, she couldn't leave without saying goodbye.

"Here they are." Drew hustled through the doorway into the loading dock, a few individually wrapped packages of cables in his hands, held up high like a prize. He was in another ill-fitting suit, and with his arm raised, the sleeve of his jacket slipped down almost to his elbow. Someone really needed to take the kid shopping. "I got you a few different sizes just in case!"

"Thanks," she said, taking the bundle from him and setting them in the back. "I really appreciate all your help."

"Anytime," he answered. She wanted to close the door so she could head out, but Drew wasn't moving to leave, and he was still blocking her door. He wanted to talk. She didn't want to be a jerk, and even though she was in a hurry to get started, she threw him a bone.

"Are you from New York?" she asked, attempting small talk.

"Yes," he answered. "Are you?"

"Nope, Kentucky." He nodded absently instead of replying, something obviously on his mind.

She waited a minute, but he still wasn't talking. That was it. That was all the effort she was putting in, if the kid didn't start talking soon, rude or not, she was out of there.

He finally spoke after another minute of silence. "Clint told me what happened to you yesterday. Are you OK?"

She smiled because he too was trying to break the ice. "I'm fine. It's really nice of you to ask."

"It must have been really scary," he said softly, unable to meet her eyes.

He was so nervous around her; she wondered if he was that shy with everyone. If he was, he must have had a difficult time in sales when talking to strangers constantly was a requirement.

"It wasn't at first," she answered. "In the beginning, it was kind of fun. I like a good mystery, and I felt like I was helping. That was nice. Then when I realized they weren't who they said they were, I was terrified. All I could think about was running."

"Can I ask you something?" he said hesitantly.

With anyone else, she would have said, "You just did." But he was so timid, she didn't think he'd get the joke. So, she just said, "Sure."

"How do you talk to people? Clint may have told you, but this is my first sales job. I've always been a tech before, so I didn't have to talk much. This job, it's so different. It's always talking and calling strangers. I get so nervous."

"Everybody does," she said gently. "I get nervous every time I meet a new client. The trick is to remember two things. One, don't lie. It never makes anything better. If you don't know something, just say so. It's no big deal not to have all the answers. It is really bad if you lie."

He nodded. "I can do that. What's the second thing?"

"Do what you say you're going to do. It's simple, but it's the most important thing. If you say you'll have the proposal to someone by Friday, get it to them by Friday. If for some reason you can't, reach out and let them know and give them an alternate date. Other than that, just fake it till you make it."

"That's it?" he asked, looking skeptical, as if he couldn't believe it could be that easy.

"That's it. Confidence comes from experience, and the only way to get experience is to do it. You'll make mistakes; everyone does. But don't worry too much about it. Clint's a good guy. He'll take care of you." She turned to pull her feet in the car, signaling the end of the conversation, but then turned back for one last piece of advice. "Oh, and remember no matter what you do, not everyone is going to like you, and you're not going to win every job. Don't be so hard on yourself. You'll get it."

"OK, thanks, Cameron." He moved away from her door so she could shut it. "What are you doing with all this stuff anyway?"

She closed the door, started her Jeep, and rolled down the window. "I'm conducting an experiment. I'm going to try to start a fire."

His face went pale, and his mouth opened in shock as he glanced between her and the gear in the back.

Cameron laughed. "Don't worry; your boss knows all about it. You won't get into trouble. Thanks again for the help. I'll see you later," she said with a wave out the window as she drove out of the garage and into traffic. Drew gaped after her, watching until she disappeared in the traffic of the borough.

CHAPTER FIFTEEN

EXPERIMENTATION IS A GOOD THING

WALKING into the police station was a challenge. She'd driven her Jeep out to Brooklyn to borrow the equipment from Clint, but since she wanted to leave her car at her apartment instead of paying for parking down by the police station, she'd gone home, unloaded the gear, and asked her doorman Joe to watch it while she'd pulled her car into the underground garage and left it with the parking attendant. Then she had to have him help her get a cab and load all the gear into it. This project was quickly turning into a workout. She was already sweating, and she still had one more move to go. It was one of the fatal flaws of living in New York City. Sometimes logistics could be a bitch.

Now she was standing outside the police station waiting for Will to come down with a hand truck to help her get it all inside. She'd called him when she'd arrived and unloaded the gear onto the sidewalk. She was sick of moving equipment by the time it was done, and people walking by kept giving her funny looks. Thank goodness the precinct had an elevator. If she had to lug all this stuff up several flights of stairs, she would've given up.

It was possible she may have gone a bit overboard, she thought, looking around at all the stuff she'd brought. In her effort to be accurate, she'd packed enough gear to test her theory in multiple configurations. She couldn't remember all the specific equipment in the systems from Will's lists, but she was sure she had enough to provide proof of concept. If not, Clint had offered Drew as a courier to bring her whatever else she needed. Despite his shyness, he was a nice kid.

"Jesus Christ," Will exclaimed as he walked up with the cart. "Do you think you brought enough stuff?"

She rolled her eyes. "Trust me, all of this is necessary if you want an answer to your problem. Now, instead of judging, do you think you could find a place for me to work?"

And that's how Cameron found herself in a grungy conference room that had seen better days, on the twelfth floor of the precinct. After lugging up all her gear, Will helped her push all the old furniture out of the way so she had enough space to work. They had a brief discussion on fire safety, and he found her a fire extinguisher from somewhere in the building in case she was successful. They'd also almost come to blows when she started unpacking the gear. She was methodical. Carefully removing equipment from precision-cut Styrofoam inserts and gently folding the plastic protection bags. She then precisely placed it all back in order in its original boxes before moving on to her favorite part. Peeling the plastic shrink-wrap from the new gear. Something about peeling the plastic felt like Christmas morning and getting a new toy.

Will was watching impatiently, shuffling and sighing. Crossing his arms then uncrossing them again like an anxious child watching someone open a present while trying to save the wrapping paper. She finally had to physically shove him out of the door by assuring him she wouldn't get any work done with him hovering, and he should go cover his side of the investigation, which was figuring out why someone was targeting those specific individuals.

Finally, alone and with all her equipment unpacked and ready, she began the first step. She pulled out a cordless drill from her bag and inserted the Phillips-head screwdriver attachment and began assembling the rack. She'd chosen a short rack, only 24U high but with the maximum depth available of forty inches. She wanted to be able to accommodate her deepest piece of equipment, the amp. That was her target. She was going to try to get it to self-incinerate.

She'd taken a break from building to examine the equipment lists once she had access to all of Will's files again. Comparing the system setups, she determined all the configurations had pretty large amplifiers and heavy-duty uninterruptible power supplies. She'd brought both. After assembling her rack, she first installed the UPS on the bottom. It was the heaviest piece, and maneuvering it into the tightly enclosed space took a lot of muscle and a little ingenuity. She'd gotten on her knees and manipulated the unit on top of them while sliding it into the rack awkwardly. After she'd screwed in the rack ears, she was sweating again.

Next, she added the amp; it was much easier to fit and took hardly any time at all. She added in the network gear and shelves for the EvryWare appliance. Finally, she added a managed power strip to the back of the rack and connected all the gear. The wiring wasn't pretty, and it went against her nature to leave it so untidy, but she reminded herself that she wasn't trying to impress anyone. And if she was successful and managed to burn it down, it wouldn't matter because no one would see it anyway.

Plugging it all into the wall and hardwiring the network was the last step. Manual labor done, she grabbed one of the mangled office chairs from against the wall and began the painstaking process of configuration.

Configuring the network was her first move; her whole theory depended on being able to access the system remotely, and you couldn't do that without the internet. Next, she logged into her EvryWare account.

She added a new location to her account and named it "FIRE!" chuckling to herself at the joke. Once she had the location set, she just added the EvryWare appliance and began a network scan. It identified all the gear she had in the rack. It was too easy.

All set up and ready to go, she opened the notes

application on her iPad and set up a record for her testing process. This whole experiment would be no good if she couldn't repeat it. Plus, if it ever went to trial, she'd imagine someone would need documentation on how this was done. Bureaucracies did love their paperwork. She listed the equipment she was using as well as the current temperature in the room. It never hurt to be thorough.

Next was her biggest hurdle. Their theory was that the murderer had used their own software to simulate an unending firmware update. And that was software she didn't have, so she had to try to replicate it as best she could. Since there wasn't a firmware update available for the amp, she logged into it and began the process of rolling it back to a previous firmware version. It was essentially the same process just in reverse. Then if that didn't produce the expected results, she could simply update the firmware and repeat. As many times as necessary until she could make it light up.

CHAPTER SIXTEEN

NEVER SCREAM FIRE IN A CROWDED ROOM

TWO hours later, Cameron was disgusted with the whole project and feeling gross. The conference room's AC had kicked on, probably in response to the A/V equipment's heat raising the temperature of the room. The cold air had dried her sweat and made her shirt feel hard and crusty. That, combined with all the dust and grime sticking to her from crawling on the dirty floor, made her long for a cool shower. Her hair was greasy and gross, half falling out of the ponytail she'd shoved it into when she'd started her work. And she was out of ideas. She'd rolled the firmware back and reinstalled it with promising results. The units were heating up significantly, just as she'd expected. But when she went to repeat the process the unit's internal fans kicked on and the machine locked her out. The amp wouldn't let her initiate the next process. It shut down just long enough for it to cool itself to a reasonable temperature, and no matter how quickly after that she restarted the sequence, she couldn't get it hot enough. The unit kept shutting down, trying to protect itself. She felt like she was watching a pot of water that wouldn't boil.

She'd known the amp would have built-in safeguards, but this was ridiculous. She longed for a copy of the arsonist's code. It seemed as if they were right; the only way to do this was to initiate a long enough update that the unit couldn't shut down to avoid the equipment's internal protections. But that wasn't something she could replicate. She wasn't a programmer; she couldn't write the kind of code necessary to make something like that happen. Not for the first time, she missed Casey; he would've been able to write a code like that in no time at all.

Fresh out of ideas, she swiveled in the chair to face the display on the wall. Using the username and password the police had posted on the wall, she logged onto the department's network and connected to the screen. She then made a FaceTime call to Bill.

He picked up quickly; she could tell by the background and his movement that he was walking on the streets of downtown Boston.

He took a long look at her before speaking. "Dude, you look like shit."

She ignored his comment and replied, "It's a fail. I can't do it. No matter what I try, the unit keeps shutting itself down. I don't think I'll be able to do this without that code."

He looked thoughtful for a moment but didn't slow his

brisk pace. "I have an idea. I'll call you back in ten."

Without another word, he ended the call, and the screen went dark. Sighing to herself as she got a look at her disheveled reflection on the dark screen, she got up and headed to the station's bathroom. She could at least clean up a bit while she waited for him to call her back.

Eight minutes later, as she was walking back into the conference room, she heard the familiar sound of her phone ringing. She answered the video call on her iPad and threw it up on the screen. It was Bill, off the streets and in an office.

"Where are you?" she asked, studying the background.

"I'm at Francois's shop. We've got a meeting in a few. We've got to do some forecasting. His sales are way behind for the year. But forget about that. What model amp are you using?"

She replied with the model number of one of the most popular and commonly used amps in their business.

"Great. Just to be clear, we don't have to do this the same way the arsonist did, right? We just have to confirm it could be done?" She nodded. "OK, so why do amplifiers get hot? Simple. Power. It all boils down to efficiency, voltage, current, and a whole host of other factors that combine to produce sound, yes, but also heat. In all, just energy. And what do manufacturers do to help prevent overheating? Simple, they add a heat sink. A heat sink is—"

Cameron rolled her eyes while interrupting him. "Bill, I'm in sales. I don't want or need a lecture on how this all works. Just tell me what to do."

He looked put out that she wasn't going to let him finish his little speech, but if she let him continue, they'd be here for days while he made charts and PowerPoints and did complex calculations involving thermodynamics. Cam just did not have the patience to indulge him right then. Maybe hours ago, when she'd first started this project, but she'd run out of motivation and she either wanted to get this disaster to work or just give up. If Bill couldn't help, she may not be able to prove the concept after all.

"Fine, did you turn off protect mode in the menu?"

She froze and began shaking her head, getting defensive. "Nope, no way. I scrolled through the menu. Several times. I read the manual. There is no feature to turn off the protection mode."

"Yes, there is. I confirmed with Francois. It's not in the regular menu, but on this model, you can get into the deeper installation menu and shut it down."

"Well, that would've been helpful hours ago," she muttered to herself.

"What was that?" he asked.

"Nothing," she replied. Furious at the idea she may have just wasted hours, and honestly, a little embarrassed that he'd figured out on his first guess what she couldn't in all that time. She had to remind herself that everyone had their strengths, and Bill was the tech. "Let's do this; walk me through it."

He painstakingly walked her through the settings and discreet menu to turn off the protection mode.

"You want to stick around for the test?" she asked when

they were finished.

"Are you kidding? After all that? Of course, I do."

She angled her screen again so he could see the rack and once again began the process of rolling back and then updating the firmware.

"All right, here we go. Test number eleven. Rolling back the firmware."

They waited in silence for a full five minutes until the software finished its cycle.

"And now updating the firmware," she announced. Another six minutes passed before the process was complete. "Here we go again. Rolling back the firmware."

She waited for the unit to shut itself down again as it had done the ten prior times she'd tested it, but after a minute nothing happened. "It's working!" she said, her adrenaline kicking back in and shaking her out of her funk. "How many times do you think it'll take?"

"I guess we'll find out," he answered, shrugging and smiling.

It took six times and thirty-three minutes before Cameron noticed any reaction.

"Bill," she said, snapping his attention away from his computer and the weekly reports he'd been working on. "I think I smell smoke."

"Well, go over there and check it out."

"What! I'm not going near that. What if it blows up?"

He rolled his eyes at her dramatics. "It's not going to explode. At the most, you may see some sparks. Now go over there and check it out."

Grudgingly, she got up from her seat at the conference table at what she thought was a safe distance away and crept over to the rack. Once she got closer, there was no mistaking the acrid chemical smell of electronics burning.

"It's happening."

Now for the real test: would it completely catch fire and ignite the other components? Enough so that it could burn a whole house down? Or would it simply burn itself out? Could they have been wrong about the whole thing? She paced anxiously around the rack while she waited. Then, out of nowhere, it seemed, bright flames began to show through the vents on the side of the amplifier. From there it wasn't long before she saw the network gear on the shelf above catch on fire as well.

"We did it!" she exclaimed turning triumphantly, hands in the air like a sprinter that had just crossed the finish line of a race, turning to face Bill and the screen where he smiled back at her.

She had one fleeting moment of satisfaction before all hell broke loose, cutting short their celebration. Beeping from the smoke detectors in the room started their piercingly loud shriek, and the flames coming from the components surged, and she jumped away from the heat pouring from it.

"Unplug it from the wall! Unplug it from the wall!" Bill screamed at her, and she rushed over to where the unit was plugged in.

She reached to grab the cord and immediately pulled her hand back, startled at how hot it was. She pulled her shirt over her hand and yanked the plug from the wall. She then rushed to grab a chair so she could stand on it to silence the alarm, but as she was getting it into position, she heard Bill screaming at her again.

"What are you doing? Grab the fire extinguisher. Put it out! Put it out!"

Oh shit, she thought, glancing back to the rack. The fire was pretty well out of control by that point, so she grabbed the bright red fire extinguisher Will had procured for her and pointed it at the flames. She steadied herself and pulled the handle. Nothing happened.

"It's not working!" she screamed, starting to panic, pulling frantically.

"You've got to pull the pin! Pull the pin! Pull the pin!"

She fumbled around a bit before she managed to locate the metal pin running through the trigger and pulled it out. She reset herself, and this time, when she gave the trigger a tug, it worked. White foam sprayed out of the nozzle and began coating the equipment and smothering the flames. It took a few minutes, but just as she was finishing coating the entire situation and the flames were long gone, the extinguisher ran out of stuff. Coughing and trying to wave the smoke away, she moved back to the chair in the center of the room to finally silence the alarm. But before she could, the smoke must have reached critical mass in the hallway, because the whole building's alarm kicked on with an automated voice repeatedly telling everyone to evacuate.

Dirty, disheveled with wet white foam all over her, she met Bill's eyes on the screen.

"Fuck," she said, hanging her head. He just laughed.

CHAPTER SEVENTEEN

OLD GHOSTS

SHE poked her head outside the conference room, using the door to shield her body and the absolute disaster her clothes had become. The mix of sweat, dirt, smoke, and fire-dampening foam had mixed all over her body to less than flattering results; she could even feel it in her hair. She watched as a steady stream of police officers filed to the stairwell, looking annoyed while exiting the building. Walking twelve flights down would suck, but she felt awful for the people on the twenty-first and highest level. That would be a workout. She looked both ways and couldn't see Will anywhere. She'd figured he would come find her when he heard the fire alarm going off, but depending on what floor he was on, it might take a while. She was debating whether to go to the bathroom and try to get cleaned up again or just wait, when she spotted the last person she expected to see there.

Freakin' Steve.

What the hell was he doing at the police station? She let her thoughts run away with her for so long that instead of ducking back inside the conference room to avoid him as he walked past her, they made eye contact. It seemed that in the months since she'd worked at SmartTech, she'd lost all her talent for avoiding her boss's notice. He couldn't hide his shock at seeing her as well. He recovered quickly and schooled his features back into the stone-faced expression with a hint of arrogance he always wore. Steve altered his direction and made his way over to her.

"Cameron Caldwell, what a surprise. I can only assume this disaster is one of your making?"

For the second time in just as many days, Cameron had to use all her self-control to maintain her neutral expression. She simultaneously wanted to shrink from embarrassment and not concede an inch to him. Something about the way Steve spoke to her always made Cameron feel like she was being called into the principal's office. She moved away from the shelter of the door and straightened her clothes the best she could. She wouldn't give him the satisfaction of knowing how self-conscious he made her feel.

"Mr. Perkins, so nice to see you. What could you possibly be doing in a police station? I heard you weren't able to assist the police. Funny, all those techs on staff and not one of them could figure out how the arsonist did it. As you can see," she said gesturing to the chaos all around them. "I figured it out. And I am just a salesgirl. What's that say about the quality of your engineers?"

"I heard you were a consultant these days," he replied, not even flinching at her dig and with a sneer that made consultant sound like a dirty word. "If you must know, I'm not here in that capacity. I was being interviewed. I was one of the victims. Someone tried to set a fire in my equipment room too."

Cameron quickly pulled her phone out of her back pocket and opened the EvryWare app.

"What are you doing?" he asked, narrowing his eyes.

"I'm shutting off my modem," she answered, furiously clicking buttons. "I can't see any reason you would be a target, and I just realized something. The only connection you have to the executives at Synergistic is the HTH incident, and that's a connection we share. I'm shutting off my network so nobody can remote in and set my place on fire. I already had to replace all my stuff after the last time I got mixed up with Synergistic. I have no desire to go through that again."

He nodded, his eyes sharpening as he focused on something behind her. She turned to look over her shoulder and saw Will headed down the hallway against the flow of evacuees.

"Well, guess I'd better get out of here as well. Lovely to see you looking so well, Cameron. Detective," he said with a nod to Will as he joined the crowd, making his way to the stairs.

She slowly turned to face Will, not missing the furious look on his face.

"I figured out how he did it," she said timidly, her head bowed and shoulders hunched in response to his expression. She was trying to gauge just how mad he was. But he couldn't really be mad at her, could he? She did tell him she was going to start a fire. It wasn't like it was a surprise. "Yay?"

CHAPTER EIGHTEEN

ANOTHER MEETING THAT COULD'VE BEEN AN EMAIL

SEVERAL hours and a trip home for a shower later found Cameron in a different conference room, one that didn't smell like smoke, mesmerized by Will's new partner. She couldn't have been more different than the stoic and life-weary Alan who had worked with him before. It would be generous to say Detective Vanessa Albright was taller than five feet or weighed more than a hundred pounds. She had a delicate and dainty face with a pert little nose and wispy blond hair. She was overtly perky and talked in a high-pitched, almost baby-like voice. And at a rate an auctioneer would envy. Cam had only spent a few minutes with her and was already annoyed. She couldn't imagine having to work with her all the time. Though it didn't seem Will minded, from the way they were communicating about the case. He was standing at her shoulder, leaning over her to read files. They were comparing notes as they waited for Captain Lovett to arrive for a briefing.

She even giggled, as she pointed to something on a piece of paper and tucked her light hair behind an ear, grinning up at Will sweetly.

Wow, Cameron thought. Just how young is she?

Her study was brought to a close as the always-brash Captain Lovett barreled into the room.

"Update" was all he said as he took his seat.

"Well, Cameron figured out how to start a fire in A/V gear remotely" was Will's first response. And there was another giggle from Detective Albright.

"I think everybody in the precinct knows that at this point," the captain replied, and Cameron felt a bit of a blush rising in her cheeks. She shouldn't have been embarrassed for causing such a scene earlier, but on some level she was.

"There have been no more arson attempts," Vanessa added, perking up on her chair like the teacher had called on her in class. "The previous attempts were spread out over several months. While it doesn't confirm the attacks have stopped, it is suggestive. The tally is still just the Synergistic board members and Steve Perkins."

Will got up to demonstrate on the large murder board on the wall of the conference room. Pointing to each picture systematically, he began to explain. "You're aware of the attack on Steve Perkins, CEO of SmartTech." At Captain Lovett's confused look and subtle nod at Cameron, he elaborated. "She ran into him during the fire drill earlier."

Cameron stared at the board in wonder. Six victims in

total. Five were the board members at Synergistic and one the CEO of SmartTech. What did they all have in common? She flashed back to that old childhood song, "One of These Things Is Not Like the Others," because she just couldn't see how Steve fit in.

"I don't get it," Cameron, said expressing her confusion. "I mean, I get why someone who had a problem with Synergistic could want to target their board. And it's quite a stretch, but I could even see someone attacking Steve. He's kind of a dick. But I just can't see the connection."

"We don't know." Will moved back to the table and began sorting through the stack of files in front of his chair. "But I think that's our next step. If we can find out what all these people have in common, we can determine a motive, and from there we should be able to find our perpetrator. I have basic background on all of them here somewhere."

"Sounds good." Captain Lovett nodded, moving his gaze to Cameron. "Is there anything you can tell us about how it was done that can narrow down a suspect?"

"I was able to demonstrate that it is possible to set those fires remotely." And there it was again, another giggle out of Vanessa. Was she making fun of her? "Which means these crimes could've been committed from anywhere. Your perpetrator could be on the observation deck of the Eiffel Tower and have started these fires. You will not be able to locate them by geography. They might not even be in New York. They could be anywhere in the world."

"Well, thanks, that narrows it down," said Will, throwing his pen down on the table. "I have no idea how to track down a murderer who by all accounts never even visited the crime scene or met the victim."

"If they aren't in New York and this crime has crossed state lines, we may have to call in the feds," said Captain Lovett, sharing a knowing glance with Will. "They have a bigger cybercrimes unit; they might have an easier time of it."

Will's jaw clenched at the suggestion of bringing in an outside agency.

"One thing is, they have to be able to log into the victim's home with the EvryWare app to do this. That's something I plan to look into. Getting an EvryWare account isn't hard. Anyone can do it by going to their website and entering an email address. However, it shouldn't be possible for them to get access to an account that already belongs to another user." At their blank looks, she elaborated. "Meaning the dealer that installed the job. No one should be able to take it over without permission. There are two ways to get around that. One, whoever owns the project can share a job with another user, and two, you could physically go on-site using the EvryWare appliance and take over the site from someone else."

"Which is more likely?" asked the captain.

"I don't know; it could be either. To add yourself as an authorized user on a job would be fairly easy; you'd just need the username and password for the admin of the original dealer. But that's problematic because anyone else with access to that account would be able to see that added user in their system if they ever looked for it. The other way is challenging for another reason. You'd need to be in the house with access to the gear to completely take it over. And it would remove the location from the original dealer's account. So, if they ever looked for it, they'd find it missing. But if the time between the break-in and takeover to the time of the fire were short, that's probably your best option."

"Can you prove it?" asked the captain.

"Maybe, but that isn't the biggest issue. The problem I have with that option is then why trigger the fires remotely? If you've already broken into the homes, why not set the fires then? The whole point of doing it remotely is so you don't have to break into the houses."

Will looked thoughtful, picking his pen back up and tapping it on the table. "Is there a way to tell for sure?"

"Again, I'm not sure," she answered, getting a little flustered. She hated not knowing the answer when asked a question, but she had done the hard part. She proved it could be done. Wasn't it their job to do the rest? "I'm going to reach out to the original dealers for all the victims tomorrow and have them check their EvryWare accounts. We'll be able to see if they still have access to the jobsite, and if so, if a user they don't recognize has access. That will tell me a lot."

"All right," the captain said as he got up. "Will, you work with Cameron on that. Vanessa, you stick to the victims. I want to know what all of these people have in common and why they were targets."

CHAPTER NINETEEN
ONE OF THESE THINGS JUST DOESN'T BELONG

AFTER a long, hot bath, Cameron's mind was drifting away from the invoice she was trying to finalize so she could get paid from her last job. She could not focus. Two questions kept pushing into the front of her mind, making it impossible for her to complete her work.

The first was Will's dismissive attitude to her pseudo-abduction. She'd brought it up again after the meeting as she was preparing to leave, and he just brushed her off, saying he'd follow up with the detective on the case and let her know. The way he said it made her doubt his sincerity. She'd heard him use that tone with others while they were dating, and it usually meant he was just placating someone. It seemed like he didn't care about her feelings at all. But if Will thought she was just going to let it go, he was sadly mistaken.

In the end, nothing bad had happened. Neither Jack nor his men had done anything to harm her. But still, shouldn't he care just a little bit? And he was a detective. Why wasn't the mystery of what they were doing there driving him nuts like it was her? She kept going over it, searching her mind for any hints they may have dropped while she was around, but there was nothing. That Jack kept his crew at a distance now seemed planned. The only thing she had given them was the printout of the processor logs. It contained a list of every button pressed in that house for the previous week, but she doubted they would be able to read it. It wasn't written in code per se, but all the identifiers were MAC addresses and serial numbers of individual components. In a way, it was like a stenographer's shorthand. At first glance, it looked impossible to read, but with the right training and education, it was easy. And unless they went back on-site, they wouldn't be able to determine which device was where, so it wouldn't help them all that much either way. Unless they used EvryWare.

She sat up abruptly, jarred by the thought. Could she find out who did the install and get into the system? She had the address. And if she could find out who did the job, she could get the client's name and maybe be one step closer to what Jack and his crew were after. She'd be a step ahead of Jack and the Brooklyn PD because she'd have a name for whoever was using that system. She smiled to herself and made a mental note to ask the crew at EvryWare.

There were a few things she could do herself. One was trying to trace the phone number Jack had given her on his business card. But that was a dead end. She found no results after entering it in several search programs. She even uploaded the picture she'd taken of him and run it through some facial recognition software to see if she could find out if Jack was who he said he was. That also produced no results. Then she'd even tried to google him. She found nothing there either. That made her suspicions he was shady more solid. Everyone had an internet footprint. To avoid it altogether to some serious work. Anybody who was willing to go to that much effort had to be up to no good.

She wondered again if she needed to tell Will about the money. Jack had paid her almost ten thousand dollars. Maybe he could use the bank information to track Jack down. Although she wasn't sure he would. Then if she didn't tell him, would it make her look guilty of something? Would she have to give the money back? Maybe she'd just keep it to herself for the moment, she decided, thinking of her mortgage payment. She could always tell him later.

Then she mentally moved on. She'd get no more work done unless she worked through the issues bothering her, and the next was, what do the Synergistic board members and the SmartTech CEO have in common? Her first thought was money. They were all loaded, but so was the majority of Manhattan, so that didn't narrow it down.

She pulled out the files Will had given her on all the victims and looked more closely at the first page in all the files. It was a cheat sheet, detailing their personal information. She pulled out some notecards and began putting the targeted individual's pertinent information on each. Once done, she laid them all out on her coffee table to get a clearer view. They were all varying ages, but all seemed to be above thirty. That meant it probably wasn't a school or childhood connection like the HTH killers were. They lived in different neighborhoods in Manhattan and New Jersey; some even had second homes. Meaning it probably wasn't a location thing. Different colleges; both men and women; some had families, some didn't. She couldn't find any real common denominator between all of them. Then she tried grouping them. Maybe there were two motives and all the targets fit into two groups. She moved the cards around and tried to pair up multiples who shared similar characteristics. No dice on that theory either.

Cameron willed her brain to work, to make a connection. There had to be some way that Steve fit into this group. Maybe there were two arsonists? One whose target was the Synergistic board members, and the other who was targeting Steve. Or was she making it too complicated? Was what she told Steve earlier at the police station true? The only connection between him and the board members at Synergistic was the HomeTech Hub incident. But that didn't explain the motive. The board members didn't have anything to do with inserting spyware into their devices, and Steve's involvement was completely incidental. He didn't even know about it until after it was over. How could any of that be a motive for murder?

Sighing, she scooped the cards up, set them aside, and went back to her work. Guess she'd just have to wait and see what Detective Albright came up with on that front.

Ugh, Vanessa. She couldn't believe Will's new partner was a giggler.

CHAPTER TWENTY

HERE, THERE, AND EVRYWARE

CALLING all the dealers who installed the home automation systems in the victims' houses felt so familiar, she almost felt like she was back at her old job at SmartTech. One exception being she didn't have to log the calls in a CRM anymore. The only other difference was that she was making Zoom calls instead of phone calls, which was kind of a downer. The world had changed, and there was no more rolling out of bed in her PJs to make phone calls. She had to get dressed and make sure that at least the part of her apartment that was in view of the camera looked passably clean.

She powered through the three calls quickly. Luckily, all but one had been former customers of hers, and the one that wasn't she had met in passing at an industry event. She'd even gotten pretty drunk with him one night at a CEDIA conference in Indianapolis many years ago. He was happy to help her. And help her they did; she was able to confirm her suspicion. Whoever had committed these crimes had done it using EvryWare. The only jobsite she wasn't able to confirm was Steve's. He'd had internal people install the system in his Manhattan apartment, and she knew she wouldn't get any help from them. She'd have to ask Will to contact them and validate her theory that way.

Speaking of, it was coming up on eleven, and she had yet to hear from him. Maybe he was out running down other leads or working with Vanessa. She wondered, not for the first time, what their relationship was. She couldn't help the unease and insecurity that thinking about their relationship brought. Were they just coworkers? She worked with tons of guys who were just friends. But they did look awfully close yesterday when they were working together. She quickly snapped herself out of that line of thinking. It wasn't productive, and she had more pressing things to worry about. It wasn't any of her business anyway. She and Will weren't dating anymore; they were barely even friends.

From her research, she'd discovered which one of her theories had been correct. The killer had shared the locations of the victims' EvryWare accounts with his own account to give himself access. It proved that he was doing everything remotely and had never been to any of the locations in person. Or at least he wouldn't have needed to. Because of this, she had each of the dealers check, and no other locations had been shared with that account. So at least none of their other customers were targets. She had the email address of the account used to initiate the attacks and cause the fires, so she hoped the team at EvryWare would be able to give her identifying information, because all she had was a generic email account.

RMBRMR1011@RMBRMR1011.com.

She stared at the address for a while. It wasn't much, but it was something. Cam was hoping it would give some clue to the perpetrator or his motivations. It could be anything or nothing. Not everyone put meaning into their email addresses. It was possible it was randomly generated, but the way it was duplicated in the domain name made her doubt that.

She squinted at the address; it was almost a palindrome but not exactly. RMR could stand for recurring monthly revenue, which was a big part of why dealers used and sold EvryWare, but that didn't feel right. Could it be initials? Could RMB and RMR be people? Maybe there really were two people working together to commit these crimes, and they'd signed their work. That would almost be too easy if they ever found suspects. She couldn't imagine anyone who could pull off such a sophisticated crime would implicate themselves so obviously. It had to mean something. Could 1011 be something in Binary? She'd have to ask a computer guy; Cam had no idea how to read that. She took out her index cards again and wrote RMBRMR1011 in thick black marker and taped it up on her wall. Maybe it would come to her; she couldn't force it.

Asking AIME for the time, she realized it was almost time for her appointment with Nate, the CEO and founder of EvryWare, and pulled up her Zoom account to log in. She threw the video up on her TV and approved access for him to sign into the meeting.

She didn't have to wait long before she saw the screen shift and Nate's face fill the monitor. Nate Scozzari was about her age and had the appearance of what in her mind was the archetype of a nerd. She never saw him without some tech or superhero T-shirt on. The one he was wearing said, "There are 10 kinds of people in the world: Those who understand binary and those who don't." His hair was unkempt as ever. He perpetually looked like he needed a haircut and a shave. But the grin on his face was infectious. He was one of the kindest people she knew in the business.

"Cameron Caldwell, good to hear from you. Although a bit of a surprise. I'm sorry to hear about what happened with you and SmartTech."

"No worries, Nate. I'm in a good place, and there's something to be said for going out on your own." She wanted to keep the conversation away from SmartTech as much as possible. Nate and EvryWare had a very tight relationship with her former employer; there were rumors before she left that the company may begin to install EvryWare on all SmartTech processors, just like most of the CE router companies did. She didn't want to put him in an awkward position and give him an excuse not to answer her questions.

"To what do I owe the pleasure?"

"Nate, I need your help. I also have some really bad news. Have you heard about a series of residential fires around Manhattan in the last few months?"

"I may have seen something about it on the news. Why?"

"Well, I've been working with the police on the case, and I just confirmed this morning that the arsonist used EvryWare to start the fires."

Silence. He didn't even blink. After a long moment, Nate wiped his hand over his face and took a deep breath. "Are you sure?" he asked.

"Positive. I talked to all the dealers who installed the systems in those houses this morning. Someone hacked all their accounts and made themselves an authorized user for those properties."

"Shit." He reached for his laptop just as she heard a knock at her door.

"Hang on a sec," she said, and he nodded absently, tapping away at his keyboard.

Moving to the front door, she wasn't surprised to see Will there with coffee cups in both hands, but she was confused as to why the doorman hadn't called up.

He must have noticed her confusion, because he said, as he handed her one of the cups, "Joe let me up. He remembered me from before." Of course, he did.

"Well come on in. I've got the owner of EvryWare on a call right now." She led him back into the living room, taking a sip of the coffee. It was perfect. Will must have stopped at the bodega on the way up. "Nate? I'd like you to meet Detective Will Justus. He's in charge of the case."

"Nice to meet you," he replied, not even glancing up from his laptop. "Cam, do you have the email address for the account?"

"Yeah, it's RMBRMR1011@RMBRMR1011.com."

"What's this?" Will asked, glancing back and forth between Nate typing on the screen and her.

"It's the email address your killer used to access their victims' A/V gear. I confirmed it with all the dealers this morning and checked the logs. It's legit. Nate's going to look it up and see what kind of information he can give us."

"Got it," Nate said. "Looks like he used fake identifying information here except that email address."

"Are you positive the information is fake?" asked Will.

"I'm sure, unless his real name is John Smith and he lives at 123 Sesame Street. I can tell you he opened the account on December 2 of last year. He had no projects associated with it until right before Christmas, when he started adding a total of seven customer locations."

"Did you say seven?" Will asked, looking alarmed.

"Yeah, why?" Nate replied, finally looking up from his screen.

"Because there have only been six fires. There's another potential victim out there."

Cameron quickly reached for the files on her table and began reading off addresses. After she'd finished, she looked up to Nate.

"Got it. There's one left; it's in Chelsea. But no worries, I can just delete the account. Problem solved. He won't be able to access the account anymore." He began reaching back to his keyboard.

"No!" both Will and Cam shouted together, and Nate froze. She gave Will a sideways glance and really wanted to say jinx, but she didn't think it was the appropriate time.

"If you do that, he'll know we're onto him, but even worse he may open another account we don't know about. At least this way we can watch it. See if any other targets pop up," Will explained. "Can you give me that address?"

Will pulled out a small notepad and copied the address as Nate recited it for him. "No name or other information here, just the address."

"Thanks," Will said and pulled out his phone as he headed for the door. "I gotta go. I'll get to the site and call for backup on the way. Hopefully, I'll be in time."

"Will," she said, grabbing his arm to stop him. "When you get there, unplug everything from the internet. He can't do anything if there's no connection."

"No!" Nate broke in from the screen. "I've got it. I can shut their modem off with EvryWare."

"Won't that tip him off?"

"No. it won't block his access; it'll just show the devices are disconnected. That could happen for a number of reasons, like an internet outage."

"OK. Cam, I'll call you and let you know what I find." He put his hand over hers and gave it a quick squeeze.

And with that, he was out the door. She locked it behind him and wandered back into her living room lost in thought and flopped down on the couch. She'd almost forgotten Nate was there when she heard his voice on the screen.

"I hope we were in time." He spoke softly.

Cameron smiled and sat back up. "Me too. And, Nate, I'm so sorry about all this." She knew what the publicity on this would do to EvryWare when it got out that their software could be used to kill people. It was a PR disaster.

"Don't be sorry. None of this is your fault. I'm not Steve. I'm not going to blame you or make you the scapegoat for diagnosing a problem. If anything, it'll give me a chance to get our affairs in order, get ahead of this. It's going to suck, but we'll get through it."

"Thanks, Nate. I can't tell you how much I appreciate that."

"Anytime. Keep me posted?"

"Of course."

"Thanks again, and if you decide consulting isn't for you, give me a call. I'll give you a job."

"Thanks again, Nate. I'll talk to you later," she said, ending the call.

CHAPTER TWENTY-ONE

IT'S ALL ABOUT THE MONEY

CAMERON didn't know what to do with herself as she waited. So, she did what she always did when bored or at loose ends: she worked. She wrote a blog post she was less than proud of for her website and mailing list. She was almost too embarrassed to post it, but she remembered the mantra one of her marketing friends had drilled into her when she started her business. To be successful you needed content, content, content. Resigned to its mediocrity, she hit publish.

She sent thank-you cards and gift baskets to some of her former customers who had given her leads. You had to spend money to make money, and so far, her former dealers had provided all her customers, so she needed to take care of them.

She finally caught up on her invoicing and then the last

dreaded task, bills. They were never-ending, and no matter how many you paid, they seemed to multiply.

She had all the personal stuff. Mortgage, car payment, credit cards, utilities. Then she had all her business stuff. Website, marketing, and so many other little expenses.

Logging into her financial software, she looked at her financials. No matter how many brightly colored pie charts and graphs she looked at, the situation was dire. She had canceled all her subscription services, so that was something. But the math did not lie. Her expenses were too large and her income too little. She needed to make some serious changes. She knew what she had to do.

She was going to have to sell her Jeep. She should never have replaced the one that had gotten destroyed by the HomeTech Hub killer's accomplice. But she had. As soon as the insurance check came in, she was at the dealership getting a brand-new model with all the upgrades. It was like a reflex. Car gets destroyed, replace car.

While having a car was a necessity when she was a rep for SmartTech, and they shared a good portion of the expense, she could no longer justify it since she was on her own. Once she calculated the monthly car payment, insurance, and parking space, she almost threw up. The total was insane. The monthly fee for her parking space was more than the rent on her first apartment in Kentucky. The Jeep had to go. It would hurt. She wasn't a native city girl, and while her mind knew it wasn't necessary to have a car in New York, something in her just felt better having one.

But it wasn't time to be sentimental. It was time to make

tough adult decisions. It was a weird security blanket she was going to have to let go. It seemed like lately, every decision she made had to do with money.

In the end, everything was about money, she thought as she finally broke her gaze away from the grim reality facing her on her computer screen. She sighed and began clearing up the mess she'd made with all the note cards on the arson victims.

Wait. She paused shuffling the cards again. *Could it be that simple?* Maybe, after all, everything was about money.

She dropped the stack of cards back on the table and picked up the phone.

"Phil," she said when he answered. "You remember that finance guy you tried to set me up with? I need his number."

CHAPTER TWENTY-TWO
MAINFRAMES AND CAPITAL GAINS

WALKING   into the Gramercy Tavern, Cameron tried to remember what Phil's finance guy looked like. His name was Eric, and they'd had one disastrous meeting at a work event a few years ago when Phil invited him, thinking they'd make a good match. It was one of the main reasons Cam always said no to setups.

When they were introduced, it was immediately apparent that Eric had been making good use of the open bar. The only thing he said to her once he looked her up and down in a way that made her skin crawl was "Ready to go back to my place?" She didn't even dignify that with a response, and so she just walked away without a word. Shuddering at the memory, she scanned the beautiful bar area. Bright and airy, it was one of her favorite places in the city to grab a drink.

There he was. Her memory of that night didn't do him justice. She'd guessed he could be considered attractive. If you squinted or had a lot of cocktails. He had the memory of a good body. He just looked a bit deflated. It was as if he was a caricature of a hot guy just set on a blur filter. His eyes were a little droopy, his face a little jowly. His brown hair lacked luster and was a dull mop atop his head that was starting to recede. Steeling herself, she made her way over to join him.

Fifteen minutes and a cosmonaut, the restaurant's finest mocktail, later, Cam was revising her initial estimate of the man and thought she'd been a little too generous. He was an even bigger creep than she remembered. In addition to staring at her boobs and mansplaining things, he'd also referred to her as "little lady." She was torn between wanting to puke or punch him in the throat, and debated internally for so long the moment passed, and she was spared making the choice.

As he signaled the waitress with a snap to bring more drinks, Cameron was sure of two things. One, there wasn't enough alcohol in the world to deal with this man, and two, if she didn't take charge of the conversation, she'd never get the information she needed.

"Hey." She snapped her fingers in front of his face to get his attention. "First, I'm never going to invest with you, so stop trying to sell me. Also, I'm not going to sleep with you, so you can cut that shit out too." The indignant look on his face would've been funny if she hadn't had to sit through a heap of his bullshit already. "I'm trying to solve a murder, and I believe there are some financial implications. If you help me put it together, I'll cover the tab." She couldn't afford it, but she figured it was her best bet to get what she needed and get the hell out of there.

His personality immediately shifted. The false charm and slimy used-car-salesman vibe disappeared, and finally a professional sat in front of her. "What do you need?"

"I have a list of people who I know are connected, but I don't know how. I believe they all financially benefitted from an event that happened last fall. I don't know nearly enough about the way finance works to figure out how. Can you help me?" He was such a sleaze it was almost embarrassing for her to ask this man for help, but she was desperate. She had some sort of mental block when it came to the world of finance. She had no idea how it worked. She knew to buy low, sell high. And she contributed the max to her 401K every year, but that was it. That was the full extent of her knowledge. She'd even watched *The Big Short* twice and still didn't understand how that scam worked. She was useless with money.

"I can try. First tell me what the event was."

"You may have heard about it in the news. The murder of Matteo Rodriguez and the arrest of the Synergistic executives that precipitated the company's pretty swift decline?"

"Sure, of course, I know about that. Shit, I had Synergistic stock. Most people did. It was sold in a lot of mutual funds. It was considered a safe stock." He snorted, and a little of his drink escaped through his nose. He wiped it away with his sleeve. Classy, he was not.

"OK, so say you knew before everyone else that the stock was going to tank. Could you use that information to make money? And is that something I can prove?"

His brow furrowed in thought, but he still had enough brainpower to stare at a waitress's ass as she passed by. "There are always ways to make money if you have insider information. Doesn't matter if it's good for the company or not. Trades aren't available for the public to see; only the SEC would have access to that kind of information. We can check the history of the market on those days and see if we can identify any anomalies that would signify the kind of thing you're talking about."

Fifteen more minutes and a lot of jargon later, she was still no closer to understanding what Eric was trying to tell her. Although judging by his excitement, it seemed her theory was correct. She was also no closer to liking him, but she did have to admit he was smart and seemed to know a lot about finance. Maybe she would invest with him….

"Eric, stop," she interjected, thunking her head down on the table. "You have to stop."

"What?" he asked, shaking the ice in his drink, trying to get to the last drop. She'd never seen anyone milk a gin and tonic quite that hard. "Am I not being clear?"

"To be fair, you're probably being very clear. But I don't understand half the words you just said. Please, for the love of God, explain it to me like I'm a child."

He paused, setting the remains of his drink down, and seemed to think about it for a moment. "OK," he said finally, reaching over to grab the blank stack of notecards she had set in front of herself when she intended to make notes, before she realized how out of her depth she was. All she'd jotted down so far were acronyms she needed to look up. "Let's say you own a company." He gestured to the stack of cards. "But you want more money to invest in your business, so you decide to go public. That means people can buy pieces of your company." He handed her a card. "That's your share. So now you only own a percentage of the whole company. The value goes up and down depending on the value of the company. Company does well, the stock goes up, you make money, and vice versa."

"I get that part," she replied dryly.

"Good. OK, so let's say you think the stock's about to go down. You don't want that. If the stock goes down, your shares aren't worth as much, and you lose money. So you want to sell your stock before the price goes down so you get the best value you possibly can. No big deal. That's how the game is played. But let's say you're one of these people." He took the cards she'd made out on the personal information of the Synergistic board members and spread them out on the table in front of her. "Then it's not so simple. Trades on your own company's stock are permitted by employees, but only during certain windows. It's legit, because it's generally accepted that you're acting on information in the public domain. Say, Matteo Rodriguez's murder. That was widely reported in the media, shares were expected to fall a bit but would most likely rebound because no company is just one person. You with me so far?"

"Yes, but how are the board members different from other employees?" she asked.

"Trading conducted by corporate officers, directors, or significant shareholders has to be reported to a regulator or publicly disclosed. Usually within a few days. For example, let's say you as a regular individual have a ton of Microsoft stock. It's your entire retirement portfolio. Wouldn't you want to know if all of the sudden, with no warning, Bill Gates sold all of his shares? What would you think?"

"I'd think something was wrong with the company."

"Exactly. And you'd know and be able to do something about it because he's required to report it. Now, the same thing. Your whole retirement is invested in Microsoft. Bill Gates sells all his shares and moves all his investments out of the company. If he's not required to report it and the next week Microsoft goes bankrupt, you lose all your money. These people are Bill Gates," he said again, gesturing to the cards. "They are required to report any significant trading they do with Synergistic stock. And they did. The Monday after Matteo Rodriguez died, they all sold every share they had. They did report it. But it took them two weeks. Also, they all filed their paperwork on the same day. That's indicative of collusion. Honestly, I'm surprised they weren't investigated by the Securities and Exchange Commission."

"OK." She nodded, finally getting it. "What about this one?" She gestured to the card with Steve's info on it.

"No idea. Was he in a position to know what was going to happen at Synergistic too?"

"Oh yeah," she answered, thinking about what Steve

knew and when. She had told him everything right before he fired her.

"It's just a guess, but I'd assume the same thing. He knew Matteo's death wasn't the whole story and dumped his stock before it tanked too."

"I don't get it. I mean, I understand it's insider trading and that's bad. But why would someone want to kill them over it? They didn't make money off of it. They just cut their losses. And it isn't like they planned it; they just reacted."

"But someone lost money on this deal," he answered. "To sell their stock, someone had to buy it. And that someone or group of someone's lost a ton of money."

"Is it possible to find out who lost the most money on Synergistic?"

"Sure, the SEC would have all that information. You'll have to file some paperwork, but you should be able to get it."

It was just like she thought. It was always about the money. Sighing, she began to scoop the notecards up and return them to her bag.

"You're leaving? I thought maybe you could stay. Have a few drinks…," he said with an eye wiggle.

Eww. And just when she was starting to like the little dweeb, he got gross again. And just like at their first meeting, she didn't deign to respond. She just kept packing her bag and adding an eye roll of her own.

"Wait," he said. "Who's Mr. 1011?"

"Who?" she asked, looking up at him, baffled. She saw he was looking at one of her note cards.

He rotated the card so she could read it. "Yeah, Mr. 1011, and why do you want to remember him?"

He was holding the card with the email address they'd found. The killer's email address. "What are you talking about?"

"The email," he said slowly, his tone implying she was stupid for not catching on. "RMBR, remember. Then MR1011. Mister 1011. I have no idea what 1011 is though."

Holy crap, the little rat had solved it.

"How do you know that stands for remember?" she asked, her energy renewed.

"There was a game show that used to be on a lot when I was a kid. The idea was they'd show personalized license plates, and you'd guess what they stood for. I was insanely good at that game. I suppose it could mean something else, but it's pretty commonly used to abbreviate remember."

She took the card from his hand and set it on the wooden table in front of her and just stared, completely stunned. It made total sense, but he was wrong about one thing. It wasn't "Remember Mr. 1011." It was "Remember M.R." Remember Matt Rodriguez. She'd check, but she thought 1011 could be the day he died. October 11. She didn't recall the exact date, but it was around that time of year. Maybe she was wrong. It wasn't about money after all; maybe it was about Matt Rodriguez.

"Thanks, Eric. I've got to go." She resumed packing up her gear at a much swifter pace.

"So, no drink?"

"No" was her emphatic answer as she rose from the table

and slipped her bag over her head and turned to leave. She hesitated briefly before turning back to him. "But maybe I will invest with you. I'll call you."

She grabbed her phone out of her pocket as she exited the restaurant and hooked a left on Park heading back uptown and almost ran smack into a pack of tourists. You could always tell who the tourists were in New York City. They were the people looking up.

She immediately called Will. Voicemail. Damn it. She didn't want to call the giggler, but Will had given her Vanessa's number in case of emergency, so she called that too. Damn, voicemail again. She called the precinct and asked for Will. When she was told he was in a meeting, she asked for Vanessa. She was in a meeting too. When she was told Captain Lovett was in a meeting as well, it didn't take Sherlock Holmes to realize they were all in the same meeting. They were meeting without her. Cameron knew she wasn't a police officer, and she technically wasn't on the case, but she had provided them their biggest leads. And she had important information, damn it. Well, so what if she wasn't invited? She'd be going to that meeting anyway.

CHAPTER TWENTY-THREE

GAMES ARE ONLY CHILDISH IF YOU LOSE

TURNS out, getting into a closed meeting at a police station was every bit as hard as getting in to see the CEO of a Fortune 500 company. Except at the precinct, the gatekeeps could arrest you. She had finally gotten as far as the homicide floor when she was planted on a hard wooden bench and told very sternly not to move. The officer that had walked her up left to go get Will, but not before stopping to speak to another officer sitting at the desk closest to her. If his evil eye was anything to go by, it wasn't hard to guess what was said.

After ten minutes, she was fuming. She and Officer Unfriendly had gotten into a weird pseudo-staring contest, and no way was she losing. She was a pro. Her competition had on a perfectly pressed police uniform, the creases so sharp she thought she could cut herself on them if she got too close. The looks he was giving her wrinkled blazer told her he was not impressed with her sloppiness. Dry cleaning had also been cut from her expense list. Now she was attempting to iron her clothes herself, and judging by the look she was getting, she wasn't being successful. She gave him the side-eye right back every time he glanced her way and gave her a dirty look. One of the good things that came from having an older brother was the ability not to blink. She could hold out just as long as he could. She would not be intimidated by that guy, so she doubled down on her efforts and refused to look away.

So engrossed in her petty little standoff, she didn't even notice Will's arrival until he stepped directly into her line of sight, breaking her eye contact with the officer. She might have imagined it, but she swore she heard a faint "Yes!" come from his direction.

His amused little grin only angered her more. "Cameron, what are you doing?"

Oh, he caught her, he totally knew what she'd been doing. But another thing she learned from her brother was to deny, deny, deny, and if that didn't work, shift the blame. Lord knows she'd been on the receiving end of that move enough times in her childhood.

"What am I doing?" she spat indignantly, standing up to move into his space. "I think the better question is why haven't you been answering your phone? I have information!"

"What information? Last I saw, you were safe at home in your apartment."

"And let's talk about that for a minute. You go running off without me and didn't even call! Did you get there in time? Did you stop the fire?"

"We stopped it, and we got the family out. But Cameron, while we appreciate your help, you're not a police officer. I'm not always going to be able to take you with me."

That reminder served to calm her down. He was right; she wasn't a cop. "Honestly, in this case, it's probably better you didn't. I had a productive afternoon. I think I figured out what this is all about, and I think I know what the email address means."

He gave her an appraising look before taking her arm, then leading her down the hallway with his hand on her lower back.

"Of course, you do. Come on."

She gave one last glare to the officer at the desk as she let Will steer her away. It was petty, but Cameron's life was such a mess these days she'd take any victory she could get, no matter how small.

He opened the door to a room she'd never been in before. Captain Lovett and Will's partner Vanessa were seated at a large and by far the nicest conference table she'd ever seen in the police station. The whole room was unusually nice. New TVs on the wall, new office chairs, fresh carpet that didn't look like it had been installed in the seventies. It even smelled new. She could still sense the lingering odor of fresh paint. She followed him in and set her bag on the table. Taking a more complete look around, she saw one of the walls had been turned into their murder board. Did they move it all in here after their last meeting, or did they have two?

All the victims were posted in chronological order, and at the end, the smiling face of eleven-year-old Ben Lang stood out from the rest. He was such a cute kid. This whole situation was tragic. To take a young life was inexcusable. But if she was right, and it was over revenge or money, whoever did this was a monster. They had even posted the new information about EvryWare that Nate provided. And right at the end, the email address with a bunch of question marks after it. They hadn't figured it out yet. When she realized she'd figured it out first, it gave her a small sense of satisfaction that she immediately felt guilty for. She thought about Ben Lang again. It was time to be serious. There was no place for vanity or egos here.

There was a picture of a man on the board she didn't recognize.

"Who's this?" She pointed at the man she didn't know.

"That's Tom Senters. He's the owner of the townhouse in Chelsea your friend Nate led us to. He's a stockbroker. No idea how he's connected."

A stockbroker; that fit. She continued reading the info posted about him on the wall. "Holy crap, he's one of Clint's customers!" she exclaimed. That could prove useful.

Done with her examination, she turned to the room. She noticed some other seats were still pulled out from the table as if they'd been recently used.

"Cameron, so nice to see you again," said Capitan Lovett, but he was looking at Will. She wondered what that look meant. Was Will supposed to have gotten rid of her rather than bring her in the room?

"You too. Sorry if I interrupted your meeting. I didn't know you were having company."

"There was an outside agency interested in the case, and they were here for an update." Will answered her unspoken question, not breaking his gaze with the captain.

"Another agency?" she asked, eyebrow raised. "Like the FBI?"

"In this case, ATF," answered the captain, finally turning to look at her.

"The ATF? Why would the ATF be interested in a bunch of arson cases?" Cameron asked.

"They're now the ATFE," piped up Vanessa. "The *E* stands for explosives. It's the Bureau of Alcohol, Tobacco, Firearms, and Explosives. Among other things, they investigate the illegal use of explosives. There was some concern, in the beginning, that these fires may have been started by some sort of incendiary device. Since now we know that's no longer the case, they won't be participating in the investigation going forward."

"Did they have anything?" Cam asked.

"They'd had some tips on some safe houses they thought the perpetrator may have been using, but nothing panned out," Will added.

"Well, I have something," she said, opening her bag and pulling out her laptop.

"Don't keep us in suspense, young lady. What did you find?" The captain looked ready to shake her if she didn't hurry up. He must have been really frustrated at their lack of progress.

"I think I know what all the victims have in common." She looked at each of them.

"That's great!" exclaimed Detective Albright, perky as ever. "Because let me tell you, I haven't been able to find anything that connects them." She trailed off, sinking back down in her seat at the disappointed look she received from the captain.

"So that's it," Cameron said as she finished outlining her theory for them. "You'll have to dig a bit into the other two victims, but all five of these had the information to profit from the Synergistic stock decline."

Will seemed thoughtful. "It's insider trading, I agree, and that's a crime. But why the arsons? That's the part that doesn't fit for me."

"That's what I said. But look at this." Cameron got up from the table, grabbed a big permanent marker, and walked to the wall. She approached the paper that had the email address on it and underlined *RMBR*. "Remember," she said and then underlined *MR*. "Matt Rodriguez. I'm not exactly sure what the 1011 stands for; if I had to guess I'd say it's October 11. You'll have to look it up and confirm, but I'd bet that's the day Matt Rodriguez died. I think whoever is doing this is pissed somebody profited from Matt's death. They can't punish his killers; they're all in jail. These people, this is all that is left. I'd suggest you start looking for someone close to Matt."

"You're right, October 11 was the day he was killed,"

Will said, giving her a smile. "Nice work, Cam."

"Well, this will certainly help narrow it down." Captain Lovett smacked his hand on the table hard enough to rattle the coffee mugs and began issuing orders. "Will, do you still have all your notes from the investigation into the Rodriguez murder?"

"I do," he answered, nodding, lost in thought. "I can also have the files pulled and call Alan for his notes too. If I remember correctly, he was kind of a loner. Not many friends outside of the executive team at Synergistic. No girlfriend. His family was all in Texas."

"That doesn't matter," Cam interjected. "Remember, with EvryWare, this killer could be in Texas, or anywhere else in the world."

"On that note, I'll leave you to it. I want lots of updates. I know you feel like since you stopped the last arson attempt, we're in the clear, but I want you to stay on it. There will be no more fires on our watch," Captain Lovett said with a stern look, making sure to meet everyone's eyes to ensure his message was delivered. While he was leaving, he moved by Cameron's chair and gave her a soft smile. "Nice work," he said, and then he left.

CHAPTER TWENTY-FOUR

ORANGES DON'T BELONG IN BEER

TWO hours and a lot of combing through paperwork later, Will and Cam finally had enough and decided a change of venue was in order. They split from Detective Albright and her giggling with her promise to dig further into the old case files and Matt Rodriguez's family in Texas. Will and Cam took the challenge of investigating his college years and his time in New York and headed to her favorite Irish bar, the one where they'd had both their first and last date. They grabbed a table out on the street in deference to the nice spring weather and each ordered a beer. Will spread his paperwork out in front of him, taking up most of the table, and Cameron pulled out her tablet.

"You take college," she said. "I'll take New York."

He agreed, sipping his beer. Cameron pulled the orange out of her Blue Moon and set it on her cocktail napkin before beginning. She started with the basics and googled Matt Rodriguez. She filtered out all the articles about his death and the aftermath. And there were plenty. Most of the other items she found were in industry and trade magazines. It seemed like his former boss, Trey Howard, did all the media for the more mainstream publications. She put her focus on the information from the time before the HomeTech Hub had launched. She'd guessed he was more involved in the publicity side of things before the success of the product, and she was right. His interviews tapered out after the HTH's release before ending completely about a year after the launch. After that, information became sparse.

"What are you doing?" Will asked as she reached into her bag to pull out her headphones.

"I found some old podcasts and video interviews. I'm going to watch them. There was nothing remotely relevant in the articles I found, so I'm taking it to the next level. Maybe he'll mention something personal in one of these. Sometimes people let things slip when they're live. It isn't like you can revise it later. How about you? Find anything?"

"Nothing so far. He wasn't a joiner. He didn't belong to any clubs on campus. He had a part-time job at a copy place, but we had people interviewed there during the last case. He didn't have any close friends. To tell the truth, I'm not sure we're going to find anything. Surely if there was somebody close enough to him to commit murder as revenge, we'd have found them by now. Maybe we're looking in the wrong place. Maybe it was a fan. Didn't he have a pretty big following in the tech community?"

"Two things. One, I don't think our killer ever intended to commit murder. Out of the seven fires he planned, only one ended in death. And while it's tragic," she said, thinking of the picture of little Ben Lang she saw hanging up in the police station, "it can't be a coincidence. If he intended to kill all his targets, he's terrible at it. That's what? Like a 15 percent success rate?"

"You said two things. What's the second?"

"Oh, right." She'd lost her train of thought. "You may be right. It could be someone that followed him he never even interacted with. If so, we're screwed. The pool of suspects would be huge. It'll be impossible to find them. Keep in mind, using this technology, the killer doesn't even need to be in the country to hit his target; all he needs is an internet connection."

"So, I guess we can rule out Antarctica," he said wryly.

"Not necessarily," she answered. "Lots of research stations down there; lots of places you can get on a network."

Will knew she was right. Since the crimes were committed remotely, there wasn't even any physical evidence they could use to tie a suspect to the crime. This was a whole different ballgame than his usual cases. He'd gotten so used to relying on forensics in recent years, he was going to have to adjust his thinking to solve this one. "We've got our tech team working with your friend Nate. So far there's no luck tracing the user. And Vanessa is going back through his old phone records to see if anything in there was overlooked. That's all we can do."

She nodded absently, draining the last of her beer. She

was going to need another one to be able to get through those podcasts.

"I missed this."

"What?" she asked, slipping one earbud out to hear him better. "Solving crimes together?"

"No," he replied, reaching out to grab her hand. "This, hanging out with you."

A million thoughts raced through her mind. They'd never done this exactly. They dated over the winter when sitting outside getting a beer had been out of the question. But she took his point, and if she was honest with herself, she'd admit she missed it too. Being with Will just felt right.

What did that mean? She wasn't the kind of girl who analyzed every little thing a guy said to her, but Will was definitely sending mixed messages. He ghosted her, not the other way around. He'd progressively gotten busier and busier, and his calls came further and further apart, until one day he was just gone. No explanation at all. But damn it, she did still miss him. She sighed as she looked down at their joined hands. His was warm and strong, and it just felt right.

"I can see what you're thinking." Reacting to the expression on her face, he gave her hand a squeeze. "That was unwelcome. You're still not interested."

"What are you talking about? I was always interested. I liked spending time with you, Will. You're the one who pulled away from me." Not prepared to have this conversation, she put her earbuds back in and began scrolling through her phone, downloading podcasts. She could still see him staring at her from the corner of her eye, but she studiously ignored him until he sighed and went back to work too.

She was halfway through her second beer when she found it. She sat up suddenly from her reclined position and pressed pause on her phone.

"What?" Will asked, noting her reaction.

"Do you still have his bank statements?"

"Yeah, right here. They're all digital."

She snatched his laptop away and typed in a search.

"Sure, go ahead," he said, waving a dismissive hand at her and grabbing his drink with the other.

She cut him off. "Found it!"

"Found what?"

"He gave a thousand dollars a month to STEM Brothers."

"What's STEM Brothers?" Will asked.

"It's a charity. It's like Big Brothers/Big Sisters of America but with a STEM focus."

"So what? He gave to a lot of charities."

"Listen to this," she said, offering her earbuds to him. "This is one of his first interviews before the launch of the HTH. He talks about how his father was in the military and deployed a lot when he was a kid. He joined the program and had a Big Brother when he was little. When he moved to New York and joined Synergistic, he was finally in a position to pay it forward. He had a STEM Brother the whole time he lived here."

Will's eyes lit. "I wonder why it was never mentioned anywhere else. It's not in his professional bio. Don't most corporate types like to show off their charitable work?"

"He was a private guy, and they didn't need the publicity.

Plus, I bet he didn't want to draw unwanted attention to the kid. I could see that being embarrassing for him."

"Isn't STEM Brothers for little kids? Wouldn't that make him too young to be the killer?"

"OK, one, I didn't know there was an age limit on murderers. And two, STEM Brothers is only for high-school-aged kids. So…"

"So what?" he asked as she trailed off.

"Shh, I'm trying to do the math."

They sat in silence for a few minutes before Will lost his patience. "He'd be in his twenties now, Cam."

"I was getting there!" she exclaimed indignantly. She was frustrated he beat her, but math wasn't her strong suit, and this wasn't like calculating a tip or a discount on an order.

"Does it ever say who he was?" he asked, taking the headphones from her.

"Nope, but they have an office not far from here. I bet we can find out. Let's go!" STEM Brothers was the nation's largest nonprofit youth mentoring program with a Science Technology, Engineering, and Mathematics focus. They would absolutely have records. She imagined a charitable organization that worked with minors would be required to keep meticulous documentation, and if she and Will could get their hands on it, they just might find the name of their killer.

As Will began to listen to the section of the interview, she'd begun packing up her stuff and searching for the waitress to get the bill. Finally, it felt like they were making progress.

"Woah, slow down there, Speed Racer," he said after removing the headphones. "It's already after five o'clock. The office will be closed. We can go first thing in the morning."

Bummer, she thought, sitting back down deflated. She wanted to know right then. The waiting part of investigations was bullshit.

"Since it appears we're at an impasse, can you give me an update on my kidnapping case?"

"Cameron, c'mon. For the last time, you weren't kidnapped," he replied, looking annoyed.

"Whatever then, have you even called the detectives in Brooklyn? Are they any closer to finding out who Jack is?"

"I talked to the lead detective today. Nothing to report. They're still working through the holding company to track down the owners of the property. You need to be patient. These things take time." Cameron rolled her eyes. "Don't give me that look. I know you're frustrated, but I'll let you know when I hear something. I promise."

"Great, let's hope he doesn't come back and kill me in my sleep before you guys get around to doing anything." She could never be a detective. They moved way too slow.

"Stop being dramatic. If they wanted to kill you, they would've done it already," he said with a wry smile and a wink. "Now that that's settled, back to us."

"Will, I'm not really sure," she began only to be cut off.

"No, you're not going to do that. You're here, I'm here, let's have this out. I want to know what happened. I thought we had something good between us."

Confusion all over her face, she answered, "So did I. I don't understand why you're asking me. You're the one that stopped calling and answering my calls. After a while, I just stopped reaching out. I didn't want to be a stalker. You'd made it pretty clear you didn't want to see me anymore."

"That's not what happened—" he said and was interrupted when his phone rang. With a sigh and a pointed glance to assure her that this conversation was far from over, he stepped away to take the call. He wasn't gone long before he returned to the table and laid a couple of bills down.

"Got to go?" she asked.

"Yeah, sorry. Got a lead on another case. I'll pick you up in the morning, and we'll head to the STEM Brothers office when they open."

She watched him go, sipping on her beer. She never minded him having to duck out to work when they were seeing each other. She understood his dedication to the job; it was actually one of the things she liked best about him. Loyalty and dedication were hot. But what did he mean when he said she hadn't been interested? Had she really given him that impression?

Her train of thought was interrupted when a tall good-looking man took Will's seat at the table in front of her and smiled.

CHAPTER TWENTY-FIVE

SO, WE MEET AGAIN

"HELLO, Jack," she said, returning his smile. She looked around him, down the street, to see if she could grab Will's attention, but he was already gone. "Are you here to kill me?"

The smile immediately dropped from his face, replaced with a look of confusion. "Why would I want to kill you?"

"Who knows," she answered, shrugging. "Why do you do any of the things you do? Why'd you lie to me to get me to work for you? Whose house was that? What were you looking for?"

"That's a lot of questions," he replied as he flagged down the waitress and ordered a Guinness and another Blue Moon for her.

"If you plan on staying, are you planning on answering any of them?"

"Are you seeing Will again, or is that just business?" he asked.

She knew this game. The good old answer-a-question-with-a-question game. She killed at this drinking game in college. Jack had no idea who he was messing with.

"How do you know Will again? He doesn't seem to remember you."

"Have you figured out who's trying to avenge Matt Rodriguez?"

How could he possibly know that? They had only found out a few hours ago. And why would he care?

"Was the house in Brooklyn related to the arson case?"

He paused their game then, an amused look on his face. Jack seemed to be having fun. "Let's call a truce," he said, taking their drinks from the server and thanking her. "How about this. Just for tonight, we don't talk about our meeting the other day or your case. Let's just sit here and enjoy the evening."

"You just want to sit here and have a beer with me?"

"Is that so hard to believe?"

"Yes," she answered.

"You're an interesting woman, Cameron. Why wouldn't I want to spend time with you? Plus, you never know, sit here with me long enough, and I might let something slip. You might just get some answers to all those questions you have."

She glanced around the street. There was no sign of the team of badasses that had been with him Monday, but given their profession, would she be able to spot them even if they were there? Probably not. And he wasn't going to slip and give her any information he didn't want her to have. That much was obvious. But he wanted something. He wouldn't be here if he didn't. Maybe he wouldn't give her any information, but it was possible she could figure out what he was looking for from her. Decision made, she began systematically powering off all her devices. Her phone, her tablet, and her laptop.

"What are you doing?" Jack asked, amused at the production she was making out of it.

"You want something. I don't know why you're here, but it isn't just to hang out with me." He started to answer her, but she held up a hand to silence him. "That's fine, you don't have to tell me, I'll figure it out. Of the few things I know about you, one is that you're well-funded. You probably have all sorts of cool toys. So, while I'm OK with sitting here and drinking with you, I'm not going to leave all my data open and available to you to copy or clone."

"Fair enough," he answered, holding up his glass. He tilted his head at her in question. "Cheers?"

"Cheers," she answered, clinking her glass to his.

CHAPTER TWENTY-SIX

DRINKING WITH THE ENEMY

"I firmly believe that all American professional sports would be positively impacted by instituting the relegation rule the Premier League uses," Cameron said, thrusting her finger down on the table to make her point, and her beer sloshed just a little at the movement.

Jack laughed at her intensity. "You've given this a lot of thought."

They'd been sitting at the table outside for long enough that the sun had begun to set in the city. The changing light cast bright reflections and deep shadows down Third Avenue in equal measure. It was the beginning of a beautiful night in Manhattan.

She nodded seriously. "I have. Let me ask you, what's the biggest problem in most professional sports?"

"I don't know, what?" Jack answered, playing along. "Injuries?"

"No—"

Jack cut her off before she could finish her thought. "Salary cap?"

"No—"

Her frustration rose as he cut her off again. "Performance-enhancing drugs? Designated-hitter rule? Concussions, scheduling, the BCS."

"Oh my God, stop," she cut in, laughing. It was weird, but she was having a good time with him. Turns out, Jack was funny.

"None of those?" he joked back, taking a sip of his beer.

"No, it's lack of incentive." She paused, expecting some kind of reaction. When he gave her none, she continued. "Pro athletes are basically big babies. If you're not in the hunt for a title, there's no reason to play hard, so toward the end of the season, players tend to give up. And why wouldn't they? They're getting paid either way. But if there was a threat of relegation…."

"Ah, I see. You think it would encourage the athletes to take it more seriously. Give maximum effort throughout the entire season."

"I know it would. All those NBA and NFL egos. They couldn't handle being kicked back down a league. The horror. I bet we'd see much more competitive games all the way to the end."

Jack smiled back at her as she rubbed her arms. It was getting a little chilly out.

"Are you cold?" he asked, starting to remove his jacket.

"Don't," she said, raising her hand to stop him. "Very

gallant of you, but I do need to head home."

He shrugged, sliding his coat back up on his shoulders. "Big day tomorrow? Leads to follow?"

"Wouldn't you like to know," she replied cheekily. "But seriously, Jack, are you ever going to tell me what you were doing in that house, what you're doing here now?"

He just smiled and reached for his wallet. "I've got this. Give me a sec, and I'll walk you home."

She sighed, disappointed. They'd had a good time chatting. Mostly about nothing. Sports, movies, and music. Generic conversation that, while fun and interesting, never veered into anything even close to personal. In all the time they spent together, he never revealed anything of himself. He wouldn't even tell her which team he rooted for.

"Thanks for the drinks," she replied, grabbing her bag and standing, a little unsteady on her feet from all the beer. "But I'm a big girl; I don't need you to walk me home."

And with that, she moved past him and started on the two-block walk home. It didn't take Cameron long to feel like something was off, and a glance over her shoulder revealed the cause.

"Are you following me?"

"I'm just making sure you get home OK," Jack answered, strolling casually not two feet behind her.

"I've lived in the city for a long time," Cameron said over her shoulder as she picked up her pace. "I can make it home all by myself."

She tripped a little on an uneven patch in the sidewalk, and Jack sped up a bit so he could grab her arm and steady her. She shrugged him off immediately, irritated. "I've got it, you stalker." She sped up again to try and increase the distance between them.

Jack and his long legs easily matched her pace, and he caught up with her, walking between her and the street. "I know you can get home by yourself, but it's the gentlemanly thing to do. Plus, a delicate southern flower like you shouldn't be out on these streets by yourself at night. It's New York City. There could be villains about."

She snorted. "The only villain about is you." They paused at the street corner, waiting for the light to cross onto Cameron's block. "And calling you a gentleman seems a bit generous."

"I'm hurt," he said, clutching his chest dramatically as the light turned, and they began making their way to her building. Stopping in front of her door, he turned her to face him. "Am I really that bad?"

"I don't know what you are, Jack. I don't know anything about you," she said softly. He looked a little wounded at that statement, but she continued. "And you did kidnap me."

"I didn't kidnap you. I just needed your help. Cameron, you have to know I would never hurt you."

He meant what he said; she could feel it in the way he looked at her. They were standing face-to-face on the street in the crisp spring evening with the sounds of the city echoing all around them. It was a moment, or what could easily become a moment, and with that realization, Cameron promptly panicked. This wasn't a guy you had a moment with. She didn't even know if Jack was his real name, and she most definitely had some unresolved stuff with Will she needed to figure out. With that thought, she took a giant step back.

"That's the thing, Jack. I don't know that. I repeat, I don't know anything about you." With that she turned and entered her building, leaving him out in the chilly evening alone.

CHAPTER TWENTY-SEVEN

PANTS ARE IMPORTANT

CAMERON woke to a pounding in her head and the ringing of her phone. She groaned and moved a pillow over her head, not even opening her eyes. She'd just begun to drift back off when the ringing began again. Growling a little, she sat up and slid on her glasses. She checked her watch while reaching for the phone. Six o'clock in the morning. Someone was about to die. She glanced at the caller ID while moving to answer it. Phil. Yep, someone was going to die. She was going to kill him.

"I'm going to fucking kill you," she stated perfectly calmly as she answered the call, sleep heavy in her voice.

"What's wrong with you?" he asked.

"It's six in the fucking morning, Phil. That's what's wrong with me. Not everyone gets up at the ass crack of dawn to go run marathons. Also, some of us had a few beers last night and need our beauty sleep."

"It's not a marathon. It's just a few miles in the mornings. It helps keep me young. Who were you out drinking with? Wait, hold that thought. I'm going to conference Bill in."

Resigned to the fact that she wasn't going to get any more sleep without having this conversation, she threw the call up onto the monitor in her bedroom. Setting the phone back on her nightstand, she chugged the glass of water sitting on her bedside table before snuggling back under the covers. She may need to talk to the guys, but she could at least do it comfortably and hydrated. It wasn't a minute later when her screen came to life, and she could see both Bill and Phil on the TV. Both were dressed in suits and ready for their workdays. It was moments like this when she was relieved she wasn't still working for SmartTech, or she'd have been in her work clothes getting ready to head out the door too.

"Comfy, Cameron?" Bill asked, amused.

"I was until some jackass called and woke me up," she replied, her voice muffled by her pillow.

"This is important," Phil said. "Have you tried to log into EvryWare today?"

"Do I look like I've done anything today?" she replied, sitting up and watching Bill tap on the tablet in his hand.

"Oh shit," Bill chimed in. "They just enabled multifactor authentication. They locked out your killer."

Fuck, she thought, throwing her sheets off and reaching for her tablet. She opened the EvryWare app and tried to log in. Denied. She knew they were going to text the phone of the admin on the account for permission. Luckily for her, she was the admin on her account. She was able to enter the code and get right back in. But the killer wouldn't be. If he tried to get into any of the accounts he'd hacked, the notification would go to the original dealers. He was locked out. He'd know they figured him out. That was their only link to the killer, and it had just been eliminated. What had Nate been thinking? She thought they'd had an agreement that he'd leave it alone. He must have talked to his lawyers. They'd probably have liability concerns. Oh well, they couldn't blame him for that. He'd given them as much time as he could.

"Guys, I've got to go. I've got to call Nate and then Will. Or maybe the other way around," Cameron said.

"Is Will the reason you look like shit today? Did you guys tie one on last night? Are you getting back together?" Bill asked in a flurry.

"Jesus, nosey much?" she replied, flopping back down in her bed. She really didn't want to get into this with them right then.

"Uh-oh, she didn't answer. That means she doesn't want to tell us what she was up to. C'mon, Cameron, you know we'll get it out of you. What did you get into last night?" Phil pried.

He was right, she'd tell them eventually so why not then? Maybe they could make sense out of Jack's spontaneous arrival.

"I was with Will initially, but he had to leave to go to work. Right after he left, Jack showed up. I had a few beers with him." Judging by the way she felt, it may have been more than a few beers. She couldn't remember. She should've kept better count, she thought as she wished for another glass of water to appear.

"Jack? The guy who abducted you, that Jack?" Bill exclaimed. "Why would you hang out with him? Did he tell you what the deal was on Monday?"

"He did not," she answered. "But he has an agenda. He showed up the second Will was out of sight, so he must have been watching us. And he wouldn't still be hanging around if there wasn't something in it for him. I tried getting it out of him, but he wouldn't answer any of my questions."

"And the answer was to go out drinking with him?" Phil asked. "What if he tried something? The guy did kidnap you."

"Well to be fair, he didn't technically kidnap her," Bill added.

"Semantics! We have no idea who this guy is or what he wants. You have no business being anywhere near him. Is this because you think he's hot?" Phil exclaimed, obviously agitated.

"What? No!" Cam replied. "I was trying to figure out his angle. The police aren't getting anywhere, or if they are, they aren't telling me. We have no way to contact him. That number on his 'business card' and email he gave me are fake. We don't even know if Jack is his real name. How else was I supposed to get any information?"

"Well, did you learn anything at least?" Bill asked.

"Not much. Strangely enough, we mostly talked about sports. He's a big soccer fan. Premier League, not the US.

But that doesn't tell us anything."

"So basically, you spent the evening getting drunk with a criminal and got nothing out of it? Nice work, Cameron; we could be fishing your dead body out of the river today!"

"Honestly, he seems like a really nice guy. I don't know what his deal is, but I don't think he's dangerous," she answered, flashing back to their time together the night before. They'd laughed a lot.

"What!" Phil exclaimed. "A nice guy? He's a criminal. You could've woken up in a bathtub missing a kidney! I don't even know what to say to you right now."

"Oh, ye of little faith. Also, don't be so dramatic." She waved her tablet up in front of the screen. "I may have been a little sneaky."

"What'd you do?" asked Bill, grinning at her, leaning closer to the screen.

"Well, I had a feeling he was trying to pump me for info, so when he sat down, I made a big deal about turning off all my devices. I told him I didn't trust him not to try to use a proximity device to try to grab all my data. But I didn't turn off everything, and I may have made a copy of the data on his phone," she answered, returning his smile.

"And you haven't checked it yet?" asked Phil, still out of sorts.

"I was sleeping! I'm doing it now. Stand by." She opened a questionably legal app on her tablet and moved to the file she'd downloaded last evening. Waiting for it to open was torture. "Here we go. It's… oh damn. It's encrypted." Nothing. She'd get nothing from it. It was all a waste.

"Damn, who walks around with an encrypted phone?" Bill asked.

"Spies, government agents," Phil chimed in.

"Or people who are in security for a living. Which is what he said he did," Cam answered, disillusioned. She sighed and threw her tablet down on the bed. It was rare, but sometimes technology couldn't solve your problems. "I've got to go, guys. I've got to call Will and let him know about EvryWare."

"Call us later with an update," Bill said. "Be careful, and just a tip if you're going to do any more video calls, maybe put on some pants first."

She looked down and noticed he was right; she hadn't put on any pajamas last night, and she was only wearing a tank top and some boy-short underwear. Holding up her middle finger to the screen, she ended the call.

CHAPTER TWENTY-EIGHT

BRASHNESS IS A VIRTUE

TWO hours later, she was getting into the passenger side of Will's car, and he was handing her a latte, which she accepted gratefully. He was becoming really handy as a caffeine delivery system. She never did get back to sleep. After her rude awakening, she'd showered and chugged a Diet Coke with some Advil before making calls to both Will and Nate. Then there was nothing else to do but wait until the charity's office opened and they could go ask some questions.

"You look rough," Will commented as she settled in her seat. "How much longer did you stay at the pub after I left?"

"Jack showed up right after you left, so I stayed and had some drinks with him," she answered casually. "And thanks for that. It's always so nice for a girl to know she looks like shit. We just love to hear that."

"Jack, you mean the guy who kidnapped you? You were out drinking with him?" he exclaimed as he slammed on the brakes a bit too late and almost hit the car in front of them.

"Can we not do this? I've already gotten plenty of shit from Bill and Phil this morning. I don't need to hear it from you too. Besides, you said I had nothing to worry about, so why wouldn't I hang out with him?" she answered calmly, meeting his glare. "And you said it yourself, he didn't actually kidnap me, so I don't see the problem."

"You don't see the problem," he muttered to himself under his breath. "Did you at least learn anything from him?"

"I did not." She wasn't about to tell him about trying to copy Jack's phone. "But he wants something. He wouldn't still be around if he didn't have some kind of angle."

"Maybe he just wanted to see you again."

She snorted, shuffling a bit in her seat, trying to get comfortable. It was starting to get hot outside, and the cheap fake-leather seats were starting to make her sweat. "That ridiculous. He's up to something, and if you and the Brooklyn police aren't interested in finding out what it is, I'll do it myself."

"Of course, you will." He was looking more harassed the longer this conversation went on. It wasn't the way she wanted things to go. She wished she could just go back in time, to the ease of sitting outside in the sun, having a beer, and just being together. "Did you sleep with him?"

"Excuse me?" She turned to look at him again, shocked at the question.

"You heard me. Did you sleep with him?"

"Jesus, Will." She rubbed her hand down her face.

"Well, did you?"

"That is none of your business!" They rode the rest of the way in silence.

"We're here," he said, pulling his car into a no-parking zone in front of a building in midtown. His jaw clenched. She could tell he wasn't satisfied with her answer. "Now please, let me do the talking."

"What do you think I'm going to do? Start accusing people of murder the minute we get in there?" Cam answered, unbuckling her seat belt and peeling herself out of the seat. Boy, she was pissed.

"No, we just don't have a warrant, and I'd like to try to get as much cooperation as we can. You can sometimes be a little… brash."

"Brash?"

"Aggressive, forceful, assertive, whatever. Just…" He paused with his hand on the door handle, taking a deep breath to settle himself. "Just be nice."

"I can't believe you're telling me to be nice after what you just said," she replied and went inside.

Ten minutes later, they walked right back out.

"Wow, that went well," she said as they exited the building. "Do you think if I'd have been a little brasher, we'd have gotten more out of them?"

They'd gotten absolutely nothing. Most of their time spent in the STEM Brothers office was waiting for their PR rep to come to the reception desk. She politely told them who their attorneys were and that they'd have to reach out to them with a warrant to get any information outside of what was found in their brochures.

"Shut up," he replied, rolling his eyes. His jaw was clenched so tightly, she was worried he might chip a tooth.

"No, really, perhaps I was too forceful. You were so right. Your way worked perfectly." They got back in the car, and instead of starting it, Will rested his head on the steering wheel. "What now?"

"Back to the station. I'll check in with Vanessa and the captain and fill out the paperwork for a warrant."

"How long does that take?"

"Depends. Could be a few days; could be a few weeks."

"That's bullshit. Bureaucracy is ridiculous. We need to know now."

"That's the way it works in the real world, Cameron. Why, do you have a better idea?"

"Yes. I know a guy who makes these cables. If I can get into the office, I can switch one out with someone's power cord on their laptop. They look exactly the same, but it's really a keystroke logger. It'll send the files to my email. Once I have that, I'll be able to tag their login info and get into their system. I'll be able to look up the information myself. We would only have to wait a few hours at most."

"So, you want to hack a charity?"

She shrugged. It wasn't that she wanted to hack them, per se. But it seemed like a more efficient way of getting what they needed than Will's way.

"No. Just no. What you're suggesting is highly illegal.

I'm going to pretend like I never heard it. And you're going to promise me you're not going to do it. I mean it, Cameron. Promise me."

"All right, I promise," she answered reluctantly, holding up her little finger. "Pinky swear?"

He rolled his eyes and ignored her offered pinky. "Here's what we're going to do. We'll see if Vanessa came up with any leads and if there's another avenue we could get the information from that isn't illegal. In the meantime, we'll reach back out to his family. Maybe they know something. It's possible he told them the name of his STEM Brother. It's not perfect, but we'll get there."

"Do you think Vanessa has anything?"

"Doubtful," he answered, starting the car. "She's a nice girl, but this is her first homicide case, and I don't know if she's cut out for it. She's extremely methodical, but that makes her really slow. She could very well find all the answers we need. It just might not be until six months from now."

Cameron nodded, half listening. She wasn't surprised he'd shot down her hacking idea. Admittedly it wasn't a great plan. There had to be another way to track the killer. Maybe there was something she could find out from EvryWare. She thought about the software and how it worked. They couldn't track him by location of IP address; none of that was tracked. But how did he know which dealers to hack? How did he know which companies installed the systems at his targets' houses? If she could find that out, maybe she could figure out who he was.

"Can you drop me back at home?" she asked, suddenly weary. Her mind was spinning in circles, and her life had been completely upended since Jack first walked into her life.

"You aren't coming back to the station?"

"I doubt I'll be much help filling out paperwork. I've got to try to get some work done today." She needed a break from Will and this case.

"Can't you do that from anywhere?" he asked.

"Sure, but, Will, this isn't my job. I've given you lots to go on. You need to take it from here. I promise I'll call if I think of anything else, but I think, this time, this is as far as I go."

He stared at her for a few moments. Much longer than could be deemed polite, but she didn't flinch, just kept looking right out the window. "OK, I'll give you a ride," he answered thoughtfully.

CHAPTER TWENTY-NINE

LUNCH

TRUE to her word, when Cameron got home, she tried to work. She set up everything she needed. She had her laptop, call lists, spreadsheet, email list. She was ready to go... but nothing was happening. Try as she might, she couldn't focus on work. Her mind was a mess. A mix of Will, the murder, Jack, and her hangover, all making concentration impossible. When she glanced up and saw an hour had passed without her accomplishing anything, she knew it was time for a break.

She found her phone in the mess on her table and texted Phil. If she was lucky, he was in the city and could do lunch. When his reply came back in under a minute, she smiled. His answer was short, only "lobster rolls." But Cameron knew that meant her day was looking up.

Settling onto the wooden bench across from her, Phil took in her appearance.

"If you're going to tell me I look like shit, please don't bother. Someone's told me that at least once every day this week."

"I wasn't going to," he said, raising his arms in surrender. "Hair of the dog?" he asked, gesturing to her beverage. A huge Bloody Mary with enough garnishes to be its own meal and a thick rim of salt and spices sat in front of her.

Cam grabbed a piece of bacon off the skewer in her drink and popped it in her mouth before she answered. "You know it. Plus, this is one of the benefits of working for yourself. I can do a bit of day drinking on a bad day and not feel guilty."

"Fuck that," he answered while flagging down the waitress to order his own drink and place their orders for the best lobster rolls in the city. Not quite as good as the ones they got in Boston visiting Bill, but you worked with what you had. "I'm in sales, practically my whole job description is day drinking."

She laughed because it was funny, but her heart wasn't in it as she stared out the restaurant window watching the people on the street go by. She didn't know when she became this mopey person, but she didn't like it at all.

"C'mon, Cameron, tell me what's going on," he said, giving her a hard look. "Something's been going on with you for a while now. Is it Will?"

She sighed; he was right. If she was being honest with

herself, things hadn't been right since she'd lost her job. She thought it was natural; anybody would get down a bit after getting fired from their dream job. But she did what she always did. Just blindly sallied forth, ignoring all the issues and just trying to move forward, hoping her problems would fix themselves if she just put her head down and worked hard. Shockingly, that plan didn't seem to be working.

"I feel left out," she said simply with a shrug.

"I don't know what that means. I need you to be a big girl now. Use your words."

She rolled her eyes at him. Phil had three kids, and sometimes he slipped and spoke to you like you were one of his children. But she elaborated as he intended her to. "It's not just Will; it's everything. You and Bill do all this work stuff without me. A few months ago, I'd have been at all those meetings and events with you. I can't help but feel left out. SmartTech replaced me; Will got a new partner. Everyone is moving forward. Just not me."

"What are you talking about? You started your own business. That's a huge step forward. I'd venture no one's moved more forward than you. The rest of us are still doing the same thing."

"Maybe," she answered thoughtfully. He did have a point. "But it doesn't feel like that. I feel left behind. Maybe it's because you all have someone, and I'm trying to do this all alone."

"So, this is about Will."

"Yes; no; I don't know." She closed her eyes and laid her head back against the bench. "It's hard to see him again.

Things were good between us, and then he just wasn't there. What was that? And then he said something about how I wasn't into him. Of course, I was into him! I wouldn't have been spending time with him if I wasn't. And then today he accused me of sleeping with Jack. What's that about? Like it would be any of his business if I was. We're not together. I can sleep with whoever I want."

Phil reached forward and took her hand, jerking her forward and popping her head back up from where it rested. "Knock it off," he said, giving her hand a shake. "This isn't you. If you want to find out where you stand with Will, talk to him. Since when are you scared of anything?"

"Boys are stupid," she murmured, taking her hand back and moving their drinks, so the waitress had room to set down their food as she arrived.

"We certainly are," he answered, eating a piece of cheese from the garnish on his drink, before maneuvering his plate to his satisfaction and then picking up his roll. "More importantly, what are you going to do about this case? You know you can't just let it go. That's not who you are."

"I know. I just needed a break," she replied as she grabbed a banana pepper from the rim of her drink. Phil took a huge bite of his roll, and she watched as lobster and melted butter fell back onto his plate and dripped down his chin. "You are disgusting."

He smiled, grabbing his napkin. "I know. It's just so good."

"I tried to walk away from the case earlier today. I told Will I was done."

He gave her a look and talked with his mouth full. "That's not you either. You've never walked away from anything in your life."

"Maybe, but I'm kind of at an impasse. I'm not sure what to do next. I had an idea, but Will shut it down."

"Why?"

"Well, it may have been just a tiny bit illegal," she said, holding up her thumb and little finger to demonstrate.

Phil laughed before wiping off the mess on his face with his napkin. "Stop making it complicated. Don't try to solve the whole thing at once. There have to be some questions you haven't been able to answer. Start there. Fill in some of the missing pieces, and it'll probably start to take shape."

She agreed and took a bite of her own roll while thinking. "I think the best thing to do is try to track it down through employees of the dealers who did the installs. I know their accounts could be hacked, but isn't it just as likely that someone did a bit of social engineering to get into those accounts? It's a much easier way to do it."

Phil nodded agreement, then laughed as she took another bite of her roll, and half of it fell out and dropped back down onto the plate.

"OK, OK, I'm sorry for judging you. It's messy," Cam said.

He just laughed and took a sip of his drink, then grabbed the pickle off his skewer and took a bite. "What's your plan?"

"I'm going to follow up with Nate this afternoon, see if the team at EvryWare found anything else out. Then tomorrow I'm going to head out to Clint's. I'll be able to do the research from there, and since he was involved, having access to his records may spark something new if that doesn't work out."

"Why not go this afternoon, bust it out, get it done?"

That was so like Phil; he really was the hardest working guy she knew. He didn't know the meaning of the word "procrastinate." Cam made a face and replied, "I have that event at the other showroom tonight."

"Oh," he said, nodding in comprehension. "Going to the Dark Side, are you? I feel so betrayed."

"Shut up; no, you don't." The Dark Side was what they called the upstart automation company that had recently come on the scene, quickly becoming SmartTech's biggest competitor. "It's good for my business. There'll be a lot of dealers there. I'm hoping to pick up some leads. I still can't believe they invited me."

"Of course, they invited you. They're going to try to hire you," Phil replied, shaking his celery stick at her for emphasis before taking a bite.

Cameron considered his words for a minute. Was the Dark Side trying to recruit her? The invitation had been a surprise. Regardless, until she sorted out her feelings about SmartTech, she wouldn't take an offer if they made one. It would still feel like a betrayal. But if her business didn't pick up, she could see herself taking it in desperation. What would it be like to compete against Bill and Phil? She pushed the thought away; that was a question for another time.

"Whatever, just have fun tonight. As for tomorrow, it

sounds like you have a good plan. Just promise me this. When all this is over, you'll talk to Will. You don't want to let your pride get in the way of something that could be good. If you don't try, you'll wonder what if for the rest of your life, and that's something you don't want."

"You really like him. You're totally Team Will."

"Of course, I am. First, he's a good guy. Second, his name fits with the group. Phil, Bill, and Will. It's like fate." She laughed and threw a piece of her lobster at him, which he easily dodged. "But most importantly, he made you happy. And Cameron, whatever happened or didn't happen between you, that's the most important thing. We just want you to be happy."

She just nodded, her eyes getting a little watery, and they finished the rest of their meals in relative silence.

Phil held the door open for her as they headed back out onto the street. She turned to say goodbye, but before she could get anything out, he wrapped her in a huge hug.

"No matter what happens, Bill and I will never leave you behind. Wherever you work, wherever I work. Wherever we live. None of it matters. We're a team. Always." She squeezed him a little tighter and wiped the tear that had slipped from her eye on his shoulder before he could see it. "OK?" he asked, pulling back to look at her and giving her a little shake.

"OK," she answered. It seemed that Phil was determined to make her cry.

CHAPTER THIRTY

CORPORATE EVENTS

WALKING into the Soho townhouse, which was the Dark Side's showroom, Cameron had to fight to keep her jaw from dropping. She knew they had dropped a fortune on the place, and she'd seen pictures. But somehow, she hadn't expected this. SmartTech's showroom in the city was nice, very high-end, very well-done, but it felt like a showroom. This place was cozy and super cool. Much more modern, and felt like a real home. The walls were painted in luxurious, luscious tones that felt rich and inviting compared to SmartTech's stark white walls that reminded her of a hospital. It felt like someone really lived there, she thought as she walked in through the foyer and into the living room. There was a beautiful, shining grand piano in one corner of the huge room, and she even spotted a glass-enclosed cigar room off to one side. This place was amazing. Her night was starting to look up; she couldn't wait to explore.

Cameron spotted the bar and made a beeline over to it. After ordering her glass of wine, she put her back to the bar and surveyed the room. She saw a few people she knew. Mostly people who worked for other vendors, but a few SmartTech dealers as well. She wasn't surprised. There was a big rivalry between the brands, and not many dealers sold both. The cold war between the companies was real.

She nodded to one of Phil's accounts she recognized, who looked like he was trying to escape a conversation with what appeared to be an extremely drunk and boisterous fellow. She planned to go save him as the bartender handed her a drink, but she spotted another familiar face standing alone in a corner.

Clutching his drink like a lifeline and in another ill-fitting suit was Clint's employee Drew. She smiled and made her way over.

"Drew."

He jolted at her greeting, having not seen her approach, and spilled a little of his drink on his sleeve. She reached behind her, grabbed a napkin, and handed it to him. He took it and awkwardly blotted at the stain on his sleeve.

"Hi, Drew," she tried again. "I didn't expect to see you here."

"Hey, Cameron," he replied, obviously flustered. He wadded up the napkin and looked around a bit for a place to throw it away before giving up and shoving it in his pocket.

"What are you doing here?"

"Clint told me to come. He thought I should meet some

other people in the industry."

"Cool," she answered, but Clint was way overestimating his employee's social skills if he thought he'd be able to network on his own. Especially in an environment like this where most everyone already knew each other. It could be hard to break into such an established group. "That's a great idea. Have you met anybody yet?"

"No," he answered, shaking his head and looking dejected. Cameron guessed he hadn't left that corner all evening.

He was painfully shy; it was obvious he wasn't going to introduce himself to anyone. She felt a bit of kinship with him. They were both outsiders here. She was the only woman in the room and a former competitor, and he was a newbie. This industry wasn't the most welcoming to newcomers. It tended to be very insular.

"No worries," she said. "I can introduce you to some people. Did he want you to meet other dealers or the vendors?"

"The reps," he answered hesitantly. "If that's okay?"

That made sense. Clint wanted him to develop relationships with their suppliers. As she well knew, relationships could get you preferential treatment. That kind of thing was worth its weight in gold. She began scanning the room, looking for some welcoming souls she could introduce him to. First, she saw one of the screen reps who was a raging misogynist. Nope, he'd bully the crap out of someone like Drew. Moving on, she spotted a wire rep who always got too drunk, bitched about his wife, and tried to grab her ass.

Wow, I never realized how many douchebags were at these things.

Then she saw them, a group of four huddled around the piano. The local sales team for the most reputable British loudspeaker company in the industry was here. They were perfect. All A/V veterans who were both very smart and very nice. They were the perfect people to introduce Drew to. Plus, she knew Clint was a big account for them.

"C'mon," Cam said, taking his arm and almost dragging him across the room. "I see some people you need to meet."

"Cam!" was the chorus that rose as they joined the guys by the piano. She felt like she'd just walked into *Cheers,* and she grinned. She loved these guys.

A half hour later, Cameron knew she'd made the right choice. The speaker guys had welcomed Drew in like he was their long-lost brother. They'd made a point to include him in all their conversations and had even gotten him to do shots with them. She wasn't sure that was a great idea, but she wasn't his mom, and it did seem to loosen him up. She felt confident he'd be OK on his own, but she still checked before she left him. She was here to try to drum up some business after all; she couldn't spend her whole night being a good Samaritan.

"Are you okay if I leave you here?" she whispered in his ear.

He nodded back, and for the first time, Cameron glimpsed what she felt was a real smile from him.

So she left him in the capable but slightly wild hands of

the boys and made her way around the space. She'd come to network, and that's what she was going to do. First stop was back to the bar where she traded her empty wine glass for a sparkling water with lime. She'd learned long ago that even if you didn't want to drink alcohol, walking around these things without a drink in your hand was not advisable. Unless you wanted every guy in the place asking you why you weren't drinking.

She made her way up the floating stairs to the second floor. In her next house, she decided, she'd have these. They were so beautiful and really opened up the space. The next level didn't disappoint either. A huge open-plan kitchen and dining area dominated the space. It was filled with mostly waitstaff. One met her eye and nodded to a staircase down the hall, so she kept climbing. The next floor were offices, where the Dark Side employees must work between showroom tours. Then she made it to the rooftop. She needed to know who their interior designer was. The outdoor space was amazing. Soft twinkle lights, lush furnishings, and built-in firepits were the first thing she saw. The space seemed to glow. All eye-catching, luxurious, but not too over-the-top. It looked livable, not like a museum. She was in love. It was like an oasis in the middle of the city.

Spotting some guys she recognized, she made her way into the fray and got on with her work.

In the middle of a lively conversation about outdoor lighting mishaps, Cam spotted one of the stalwarts of the A/V rep community alone at the corner of the bar nursing a drink. He looked down, and since it was rare to see the man alone, especially without his ever-present smile, she made her way over to see what his deal was.

"Hey, Mr. Cole," she said in greeting as she watched the bartender replace his empty glass with a fresh one. It was, she suspected, his usual bourbon neat. "What are you doing over here all by yourself?"

John Cole was the owner of the longest-lived A/V rep firm in the New York area. He was probably pushing seventy, though Cam didn't know his age for certain. He'd been an advocate for independent rep firms since Cam had joined the industry. He'd served on the board of almost all the industry groups at some point. He was a living legend, and Cam always enjoyed an opportunity to chat with him. She figured he'd always thought of her as a novelty and not a peer, but he was still kind to her every time they crossed paths.

"Nice to see you again, Cameron. Let's get you a drink." Cam didn't argue when, at his signal, the bartender placed a bourbon in front of her. She just dutifully took a sip and smiled. "No more of that Mr. Cole shit, kid. You make me feel old. It's just John."

"You okay, John?" She could tell by his speech he'd had a lot to drink already, and he showed no signs of slowing down.

If his deep sigh was anything to go by, John was not doing all right. "I lost a line today. Thirty years I've represented those fuckers, and they fired us today. Thirty days' notice. In an email. A fucking email. Couldn't even bother with a phone call. This business is going to shit.

There was a time when relationships meant something. If a company had to make a change, the very least they did was tell you to your face like a man. But not these little pussies they've got running the businesses today. No respect. These corporations. They hire these twenty-five-year-old kids right out of business school. I've got shoes older than some of these executives. These kids with their spreadsheets and their analytics. They have no comprehension of what goes into building a relationship with a customer. Little fuckers.

"It was an anchor line. I won't be able to make up the revenue. I'm going to have to let my team go." He paused to drain his drink like it was a shot and then motioned to the bartender for another. "I'll be okay; it's about time I retire anyway. But it's my guys I'm worried about. They've been with me a long time. Long time. A few of them had hoped to take over the business. Now they'll have to look for other jobs. Only thirty days' notice, those little pricks."

"I'm so sorry," she said. It was heart-wrenching to see a good man brought so low. "Can I help at all?"

"You're a good kid. Thanks for asking, but no. You've got your own shit to worry about. I heard what Steve did to you, that stupid fuck. How's the consulting business going?"

"It's going." Tonight was most definitely not the night to ask for John's advice about her prospects. He'd always made an effort to not curse in front of her, a sweet but totally unnecessary gesture. Hell, she had a mouth like a sailor at the best of times, but she couldn't hold a candle to John tonight. Those guys must've really pissed him off. She was dying to ask him what line it was but couldn't come up with an appropriate way to be nosey, given his mood. No matter, she'd find out soon enough. Nothing in this industry stayed secret for long.

"Hmm. You're a smart girl. You'll be fine." He raised his glass, and she clinked it before taking a drink and smiling sadly at him. "Stop looking at me like that."

"Like what?"

"Like you feel sorry for me. I've had a good run. No shame in that."

"No, there's not," she agreed, trying to think of a way to cheer him up. "Do you need a hug?"

The side-eye he gave her through his bushy white eyebrows was epic. "Don't you dare try to hug me."

"C'mon," she said, seeing a twitch in his mouth at her teasing, throwing her arms open wide. "Let's hug it out."

She threw her arms around his waist and gave him a big squeeze. He didn't move to return the gesture at all. "Kid, if you don't let go of me in two seconds, I'm going to dump this drink on your head."

She squeezed again before letting go and moving back a few steps to get out of his range. She had no doubt he'd make good on his threat. "And that's the problem with the elderly today; they don't have any respect for good bourbon."

He burst out laughing, and Cam felt her heart lighten a bit.

Making her way back down the stairs an hour later, Cam was feeling pretty good about herself. She hadn't really wanted to make the effort to get dressed up and go out. With everything going on with Will, Jack, and the arsons, she was distracted. But she was glad she had. She'd made some connections with dealers she'd never met and had some good leads on potential work. And maybe she'd helped cheer up an old friend. All in all, a very successful outing. And she reminded herself as she headed down the last staircase this was exactly why she couldn't continue to get mixed up with Will and his cases. She needed to keep focused if she was going to make her business a success. And she really wanted that. She wanted to still be attending these events in thirty years, having run a successful business just like John. She should be so lucky. But she still knew deep down that she had to see this one through. She couldn't leave it unfinished.

Finally reaching the bottom of the stairs, she stopped in surprise. The audio guys had taken over the piano and were conducting an impromptu singalong. They were leading the room full of other guests in a very lively rendition of "Piano Man." She laughed to herself, wondering how many shots they'd had as she made her way to the exit. Trying to say goodbye to them now would be impossible. She'd get pulled into the madness, and they'd have her singing with them for hours if she went over there. Those guys were great, but they liked to party. She knew without a doubt they'd be the last people to leave, and she needed to get home. She had big plans for the next day. She was finally going to get to the bottom of all of this so she could put it behind her. Then she'd figure out where things stood with Will and maybe put that behind her as well.

"Cam," she heard as soon as she'd reached the door.

She turned and saw Drew coming toward her. "Hi," she said. "Having fun with the guys?"

He nodded. "Yes, they're great. I just wanted to say thank you before you left. I wasn't doing all that great before you came, and I was thinking of leaving. Thank you for helping me out. I really appreciate it."

"No problem, just watch yourself. You don't have to match them drink for drink. They're professionals. Own your amateur status and act appropriately."

He bobbed his head and bounced back into the party. From the sounds of it, they'd moved on to "Tiny Dancer." Her warning might have come too late, but she wasn't going to worry about it. He was an adult; he could make his own decisions. And anyway, that's how you learned. It had taken her many wild nights out and painful mornings for her to learn her lesson about trying to go drink for drink with those guys.

She laughed to herself a bit at the memories before heading out the door to find a cab. It was a successful night all around. New potential clients, and she did a good deed. You couldn't ask for more than that.

CHAPTER THIRTY-ONE

ARTISANAL AND ORGANIC

CAM got up early the next morning, and before doing anything else, even leaving her bed, she sent follow-up emails to all the potential new clients she met last night. Then she added them all into her email-marketing database. She had a flashback to one of her former mentors telling her that nothing in business was more important than follow-up. He always said you couldn't wait for things to happen; you had to make them happen. After completing her task, she got up, got dressed, and prepared to head to Clint's. She had a murder to solve.

It took an hour for her to get to AVSDAM. It had only taken fifteen minutes on the subway to get from Manhattan to Brooklyn. The rest of her travel time was spent making a special stop. Some might think it a waste of time, but she knew better. She nudged open the large glass door with her hip and made her way into the office, hands full with two large bakery boxes, the product of her side trip. She saw Clint standing behind the counter with Drew, going over some paperwork, and Clint's face perked up when he saw what she was carrying.

"Is that what I think it is?" he asked, coming out from behind the divider to take the boxes from her.

"Only the best for you," she replied, handing the donuts over. Well, more specifically the artisanal, organic Cronuts she picked up. They were in Brooklyn after all. "Hi, Drew."

Clint placed the box on the shelf, removed one of the treats, and immediately took a massive bite. She handed him a napkin, which he took gratefully. "You want something." Clint glanced between her and the bakery boxes, his eyes sparkled with intrigue. "This is a bribe."

She gave a glance to Drew and said, "Yes. Can we talk privately?"

"Sure," he answered with a sardonic smile. "But no need. He knows all about your investigation. Who do you think billed the police for all the equipment you set on fire?"

She winced. "My bad, but I did tell you that might happen."

"Oh, it's not a problem. I charged them full retail. I even charged them labor for Drew's time helping you load it all up. It was a great deal for me. Margin on audio components is huge."

"Fine, I want to know how the killer knew which dealers did the installs in the victims' homes. We're not security people. There aren't little signs on the front of their houses or the windows saying, 'This house has a smart home by....' So how did he know which EvryWare accounts to hack?"

"That's an excellent question. How can I help?"

"Can I borrow your office for a bit? I want to do some digging to see if any of the dealers posted anything or wrote any articles for trade magazines that could've let someone know they did the install."

"Sure, but you didn't need to come all the way out here or bring these delicious bribes for that. What do you really want?"

"Can you give me access to your EvryWare account? I want to see what data I can get from you before I start making calls to the other dealers affected. There are only four of you in total since some did multiple installations. I want to see if there is any commonality. Anybody who would've had access through all of you."

"Good call. I'll set you up in my office; just let me know if you need anything."

"Cool, thanks." She moved to grab her bag from where it'd been sitting on the ground, but Clint beat her to it. What a gentleman, she thought, rolling her eyes.

"Jesus," he said taking in the weight of her pack. "What the hell do you have in here?"

"Clint, I could run a third-world country with the equipment I have in my bag. Don't judge. And Drew, make sure you grab one of these Cronuts. The hype is real. They are awesome," she said, smiling over her shoulder as she followed Clint back to his office.

He froze at her words like a startled bunny and sort of

nodded before shuffling away from her, and she wondered what that was about. She thought they'd made a connection last night. Maybe he was embarrassed by his behavior, even though he had no reason to be. She shrugged off the response and continued on her way. He was sort of a weird kid.

CHAPTER THIRTY-TWO

THE DEVIL IS IN THE DETAILS AND TURNS OUT EVRYWARE ELSE AS WELL

"CAMERON!" came the shout from the office door, and she jerked her head up, surprised at the sound. Clint was staring at her.

"Jesus, what?" she asked.

"I've been calling you for five minutes."

She reached up and pulled her earbuds out and shook them in his general direction. "I couldn't hear you."

"I can see that. I'm going to run out for some food. Do you want some dinner?"

Dinner? She glanced at her monitor. Oh wow, it was almost six o'clock. She'd been sitting in this office all day; she'd been so absorbed she hadn't even had lunch. "Yeah, that would be great. Where are you going?"

"Just up the street; there's a great Indian place. Want some curry?"

"That sounds awesome. Just grab me some chicken, and pretty spicy, please."

"Sure, have you found anything?"

"Maybe. There's something weird here. I need your employee records to confirm, but all the other three dealers have had a short-term employee pop up on the books for only a month or two in the last year. The names are always different, and I've gotten varying descriptions, but it could be the same guy. It would explain everything. I mean, at least how he was able to get into everybody's EvryWare software."

"That's awesome. I'll get that employee list for you when I get back. See you in a few."

"Later," she replied distractedly, diving back into the lists she'd created. She needed to call Will. She'd mapped a single suspect who looked to be moving through the affected dealers in a fairly linear pattern.

It started right before Christmas when a man named Jeremy Portman got hired at the first dealer as a tech. Dealer one was the integrator for the first two Synergistic board members targeted. He left right after the New Year. A commercial company in the city was the next on her list. They had a new hire that only lasted six weeks. They did the installation for the next victim. Then dealer three showed a new hire for another month-long stint as a tech. They had victims four and five on their books. All the employees had different names, but it was too big a coincidence; it had to be the same man. From there he disappeared. She'd check with Clint when he got back to see if he'd hired any new techs recently. It was a slightly confusing scenario, so she'd spent the afternoon making charts and a spreadsheet to make it easier to follow.

All she had left to do was figure out how he'd gotten into Steve's account. Typically, Steve used in-house SmartTech employees to do his installations. Why pay someone when you can get your people to do it for free? But maybe he'd contracted it out. Or possibly given access to his system to someone for testing. She just didn't know who she could ask. She didn't want to get Bill and Phil involved in anything that could threaten their careers, and she didn't have a strong connection in tech support anymore. Not since Casey died. She'd figure it out. No reason to get discouraged. She was on the right track at least.

She needed to call Will, she reminded herself as she checked her phone. Nothing from him all day. That could not be good. Either he was leaving her out of the investigation again, or they hadn't made any progress. It could be he was working on other cases. He always did pull a crazy caseload. She was familiar with multitasking, having always juggled multiple projects, but Will's job was murder. And it felt somehow crass not to give murder victims your full attention, especially when that victim was a child, like in this case.

She heard a noise at the door and spoke without looking up. "That was fast. What'd you get me?" When she didn't receive an answer, she glanced up.

Drew was standing in the doorway, a terrified look on his face and a gun in his hand. At the sight, it all clicked, and Cameron was pissed. Once, just once, she would like to figure out who the killer was before they had the opportunity to confront her. Her mind flashed back to the pain she'd felt getting stabbed last year, and her blood ran cold. But Drew wasn't Brandon Reese, and he made a far less intimidating figure than Brandon had, even with the gun in his hand. He looked petrified to be holding that gun. His face was pale and seemed bloodless. Washed out and sallow, he was almost like a ghost in the doorway. His motions were jerky and harsh; it looked like he wasn't fully aware of his own actions.

She ran through the little she knew about him and confirmed none of his crimes were committed with any physical contact. He'd done everything remotely. She was 100 percent sure she could take him in a fight if it came to that. The gun was the wild card, but looking at him, she couldn't imagine he had it in him to shoot her while looking her in the eye, but she wasn't willing to bet her life on it.

She couldn't run; he was blocking the only door. She could hide behind the desk, but he could just walk around it and shoot her then. And he'd be a more accurate shot at such close range. He was too far away for her to charge him. He would be able to get a shot off before she could close the distance between them. She was so screwed. Her best bet was to try to talk him out of hurting her.

She made a subtle move, sitting up a little straighter in her seat while simultaneously sliding her phone off the desk and dropping it into her lap. As inconspicuously as possible, she dialed Will. Thank God for the favorites page quick access. Two more button presses and she had turned down the volume on the phone and set it on speaker. That way Will would be able to hear them, but Drew wouldn't be able to hear Will and give away her one hope at getting help. She'd never taken her gaze off Drew, and he didn't look like he'd noticed. He looked completely panicked.

"So, it was you?" she asked softly, keeping her voice gentle, even, and calm. She didn't want to startle him into shooting.

"You were going to find out. I heard you before, talking to Clint. You figured out what I did. With the jobs, how I did it," he said, his voice high-pitched and slightly manic. He sounded like he was close to tears. "Why'd you have to be so nice to me? Why couldn't you just let it go? The police were never going to figure it out."

"I did, but I still don't understand why. You were Matt Rodriguez's friend, right? His STEM Brother?"

He nodded. "I was. He was such a good guy. He didn't deserve what they did to him."

"I know," she answered. "I was there. I helped put them in jail." Maybe demonstrating she had helped Matt too would make him less likely to shoot her. "But, Drew, the people who killed him have all been punished. It still doesn't explain why you did this. You killed a child."

"I didn't mean to kill anyone!" he shouted, running his fingers through his hair. He was beginning to look more agitated. That wasn't the right direction to go. She made a mental note not to bring up the murder again. "It was just supposed to be the fires. They shouldn't have profited from Matt's death. It was callous, and it was cruel. I just wanted to do the same thing to them. I'd just burn down their houses. Make them pay for what they did. That kid wasn't supposed to be there! I made sure. I used EvryWare to get into their systems. I checked. I made sure the houses were empty. It wasn't supposed to happen that way; nobody was supposed to die."

"I know, and the police know it too. That's why you didn't set any more fires after that, right?"

"Yes, exactly. I couldn't do it again. Not after that." He nodded furiously; his eyes were a little unfocused, and he was looking off into the distance with the gun hanging loose by his side. She wondered if he'd given up the idea of shooting her. She shifted a bit in her seat to test that theory. His eyes snapped back to meet hers, and his hand tightened on the gun.

"I get wanting to hurt the board at Synergistic, but what did Steve and the stockbroker have to do with it?"

"Same thing. Your boss Steve was a day late on the action. He was behind the Synergistic team but still ahead of the general public. And Tom Senters too. He's Steve's broker. He figured out what was going on when Steve called him to make the trades. He just acted on his information. But I never set the fire in his house. I couldn't do it again, not after the kid died."

"His name was Ben Lang. He was eleven years old." She knew it was a bad idea, but she didn't like the way Drew had seemed to convince himself he hadn't done anything wrong. She wanted to remind him; she wanted to make him feel what he had done.

"I know. Don't you think I know that?" He was actively crying. "I just wanted to cost them money. That's all they care about anyway. They don't care about people. They didn't care about Matt. Even after everything he did for them. He made that company, and as soon as he died, none of them could wait to profit from it."

Technically that wasn't true. They didn't profit in the strictest sense of the word. They just minimized their losses. But she took his point; she wasn't going to argue semantics with him. And as long as he was talking to her, he wasn't shooting. "But you cared. He was your friend."

"He was more than that. My dad was in the military, just like Matt's. He was never home, and my mom worked all the time. Matt was there for me when no one else was. He didn't have any family in town. He was my big brother."

"How come no one knew about you?"

"I don't think he consciously hid it, but he did keep me away from Synergistic. I don't think it was a part of his life he was very proud of. I think he needed something to be separate, to be real. And I know he thought those people were his friends, but I never did. And look at what happened. I was right about all of them; they were evil."

She took his pause and reflection as an opportunity to glance down at her phone. It was dark. The call was ended. Will must not have answered. The call would've rolled to his voicemail so he would've heard some of the conversation, but she couldn't count on him checking his messages anytime soon, if he even remembered how. And even if he did, he was still in Manhattan, and it would take time. Too much time to get to Brooklyn from there. She couldn't count on help from Will.

"Tell me about him."

"What?" he asked, his long limbs jerking a little, clearly surprised by the question.

"Tell me about Matt. I never met him." *I'm just trying to keep you talking, you idiot.* "I mean, I heard a lot about him during the investigation last year, but I never got to talk much to anyone that knew him personally."

"He was so cool." He seemed a little more relaxed as they talked about a friend and not his crimes. "He helped me with school. Once we built a robot together...," While Drew droned on, Cam was trying to come up with an escape plan. Could she count on help when Clint got back with dinner? Or would that just compound the situation and startle Drew into action? Knowing Clint's proclivity for drinking and socializing, it was more than likely he'd take a seat at the bar while waiting for their order and be there longer than intended. It had happened before. She couldn't risk Clint getting hurt too. She needed to make a move before he came back.

Drew's obvious inexperience was the one thing she had working for her. He was clearly uncomfortable with the weapon. She just needed a distraction. Something to draw his attention for a few seconds. Discreetly, she darted her eyes around Clint's desk, looking for anything that would help. Paper, pens, notebook, more paper, a stress ball. Nothing useful. Then she spotted it. Sitting on the corner of his desk was the tabletop touchscreen that controlled the whole office. She could turn on the music loud in another room, and hopefully that would startle him enough to draw his attention. He was jumpy enough; it would probably buy her enough time to do something. But would it be enough? She tried to calculate the odds in her head, but math was never her strong suit, so she just decided to go for it. A small chance was better than sitting and waiting for him to work up the courage to shoot her. She wasn't going to lie down and die for this asshole.

She took a minute to gather her nerve. Still, she never took her eyes from Drew and nodded at what seemed like the appropriate times while he waxed on about Matt and his innumerous virtues. She needed to psych herself up. It was going to get physical, and if scrapping with her brother as a kid had taught her anything, it's that if you were going to fight, you had to commit. She had to make herself mad.

Setting fires in rich people's houses didn't piss her off so much, they were insured after all, but this guy killed a kid. She was taking him down.

She leaned forward and placed her arms on the desk. Nodded along, selling her interest in Drew's story about him and Matt going to a museum. She left her right arm in its place while she slowly moved her left hand over to the touchscreen. She was fortunate that Clint had sprung for the ten-inch model, so it obstructed her movements. Using her peripheral vision, she touched the screen to activate. She then selected the theater and turned the volume up as loud as it would go. Way past eleven. With a deep breath and a firm commitment to her next actions, she hit Play.

Music loudly blared from the front of the store, and Drew's reaction was immediate. He jolted with shock, almost dropping the gun in his surprise as he whipped his head around to look through the doorway.

Cam didn't waste a second. As soon as she hit Play, she was on her feet. She used the big leather executive chair as a step stool to the desk and then sprang at him with all her might. Drew quickly recovered from the sound of Mozart booming from the theater. He turned back and panicked at the sight of a flying Cameron Caldwell coming straight at him. He didn't even raise the gun.

She landed on him in a flop and immediately felt a sharp pain, like a bee sting in her left thigh. It burned, but she didn't slow down or even hesitate. Her arms were tangled with Drew's, and she got her right free first. With everything in her, she punched him straight in the face. The sound he made at the contact made Cameron's guts clench. From the crunching noise and his whimper, she knew she had hurt him. She still didn't stop; hesitation could get her killed. She'd freed her left hand and again threw a swift punch into the side of his face. She kept going, swinging like a banshee. Fast, furious, and out of control, she couldn't hear anything. Her vision tunneled. Her body was hot, and all she saw was red.

By the time she came back to herself, she was exhausted. Her arms felt like they weighed a thousand pounds. She'd completely worn herself out. It felt like hours had passed, but it had probably only been minutes. She rolled off

Drew's limp body and onto her back on the plush carpet. Her breathing was heavy, and she found it hard to swallow. Her throat was so dry. She took a deep inhale and looked to her left. Drew wasn't moving. She reached out and slid the gun out of his hand and away from his body.

He hadn't even flinched. Did she kill him? Was that even possible? Surely, she couldn't kill a man with her bare hands. Cameron lay prone on the floor, flat on her back, and just watched him as she tried to catch her breath. Was Drew breathing? He was so still, and there was an unnatural quietness in the room. The only noise came from the music blaring in the theater down the hall. But it sounded so far away, like it was coming from another world, not the next room. Her heart sank as an empty feeling crept into her gut, and the fear she felt was almost a tangible thing. Had she killed a man? She couldn't, wouldn't think it.

She unconsciously reached up to wipe away the tears that were suddenly streaming down her face. She couldn't seem to control it or make it stop. Everything was just pouring out of her; all the emotion of the last few days was finally releasing. And then, out of the corner of her blurry eye, she saw Drew's chest move. He wasn't dead. Tears fell out of her in a torrent. She was sobbing violently now, snot coming out of her nose. Shaking, she sat up and wiped her face. She was a mess. All the fear, all the rage she felt had just exploded out in a flood of emotion. It seemed to go on forever.

Then, as suddenly as it began, it stopped. She sniffled a bit as she felt arms wrap around her from behind, and she heard a soft "shh, shh." She curled into the comfort and let it sweep her away.

CHAPTER THIRTY-THREE

DÉJÀ VU ALL OVER AGAIN, AGAIN (OR COME HERE OFTEN?)

SHE woke up to the stark whiteness that could only mean she was in a hospital room. She groaned as she tried to sit up and take stock of herself. Her mouth was dry and scratchy; so were her eyes. She needed some drops or to take her contacts out ASAP. Her eyeballs felt raw. There was no telling how long they'd been in. Her head felt OK, all limbs were attached, but there was a dull throbbing in her left thigh.

She fumbled her way into a seated position and looked around. She was in a private room. She reached for the plastic pitcher of water on the bedside table and poured herself a glass. She knew you were supposed to sip, but she drank it down greedily. Every drop. Then poured herself another one. She felt like she has spent a week in the desert without any water, she was so dehydrated. So, she did her best camel impression and chugged the second glass down too.

There was a pretty flower arrangement on the table. Bright purple blooms that were full and light. She reached over and softly ran her fingers through the petals, searching. No card. Hmm. There was a chair pulled up to her bed, so someone must have been here. She wondered who.

Cameron moved again to see if her phone or her bag had made it into the room, when she felt an awful pull on her thigh. She hissed in pain as she moved the thin bedsheet away and saw a thick layer of gauze wrapped around her leg.

She was staring at it, baffled, when she heard a voice from the doorway. "You got shot."

"Bill?" she asked as he moved further into the room, settling himself in the chair and reaching over to take her hand. "What're you doing here? Why aren't you in Boston?"

"I repeat. You got shot." He ran his free hand over his face. "Jesus, Cam, you've got to stop doing this shit."

"Like I meant to; I didn't shoot myself!" she exclaimed, getting defensive.

"No, you just did a swan dive off a desk onto a guy holding a gun."

"How do you know that?"

"Oh," he said, grinning. "Your boy Clint had cameras in his office. I saw the whole thing."

Wow, that was embarrassing. That meant he saw her completely lose it too. "I feel like we've been here before," she said sheepishly.

"Should I tell you the usual? What happened, how you got here?" he asked, humor evident on his face.

"Yes, please."

"To start, they arrested Drew, so you don't need to worry about that. He's in a room here too, an officer with him. You really did a number on that guy. You broke his jaw. They had to wire it shut." She looked at her hands. They were scraped, and she could tell they had been treated. A little bruised possibly, but it didn't feel like she had broken anything, she thought as she flexed them, testing the damage. She probably owed her brother a thank-you for teaching her how to throw a punch properly. "Will was here too. He had to run out, but he should be back in a bit to fill you in on the rest of it. I guess he got a voicemail from you and called a buddy in the Brooklyn police department. They went to the store and found you."

She nodded and settled back into the pillow, suddenly sleepy. "Get some rest. I'm going to go crash at your place. I'll be in town for a few days. We have quarterly meetings at the office next week, so I'll be around for a bit."

"OK." She smiled, pulling the thin sheet and scratchy blanket up to her chin. "Tell me something funny before you go."

"Something funny?" he asked. She nodded. She needed something else to think about besides the crunching noise she'd heard when she hit Drew's face. Bill thought for a minute. "The new girl in marketing wants us all to refer to the dealers as technologists."

"What?" she said, laughing.

"Yep, and every time anyone says 'dealer' on a call or in a meeting, she interrupts and says 'technologists' and makes whoever said it repeat it. Meetings are taking forever."

She smiled to herself and closed her eyes.

When she woke again, it took her a minute to figure out where she was. She finally placed herself in the hospital, then moved on to the next mystery. Whose feet were propped up on her bed? She followed the long limbs up to a torso with arms crossed over it and finally to Will's face staring back at her. He was reclining in the chair she'd spotted earlier.

"Hi," she said, her voice still rough from sleep.

"Hey," he replied softly. "How are you feeling?"

"I got shot."

"I know," he answered, grimacing. "I'm so sorry."

"It's not your fault. I didn't think he would shoot me. He looked so scared holding that gun. I didn't think he had the balls."

"He was scared," Will replied, taking his feet off the bed and leaning forward to take her hand. "I talked to him. He was terrified. He'd never been in a fight. Not even as a kid. When he was setting the fires, he was removed from the violence, the physicality of it. I don't think it was real to him. It was like a movie or a video game. He didn't even watch the blazes or the footage on the news. He just hit a button and moved on. It all changed when the Lang kid died. It became more real and sent him into a tailspin."

"It feels like it all just got out of hand for him."

He nodded. "Exactly. And it freaked him out when you

came around. When you took all that gear to the police station, he knew what you were doing. And then when he heard you talking about getting those employee lists at Clint's, he knew he was done. His plan was to shoot you and run. He didn't want to. You'd been so nice to him, but he was going to do it. Don't know how nice he thinks you are now, after you beat his face in," he said with a chuckle.

She gave him a wry look at the joke. "I don't know if he could've done it." He gave a sharp look to her leg. "No, I mean, I know he shot me, but I jumped him. I think he just reacted. I don't know if he could've pulled the trigger on purpose. I don't think he had it in him."

"Well, I'm just glad you took the initiative. It's better not to have had to find out."

"I guess you saw the video too?"

"Honey, everyone has seen that video. Clint set it to music and posted it online. You've gone viral," he said with a laugh. "It's pretty awesome. He even has a cut of you jumping off the desk in slow motion."

"Great," she said sarcastically. The whole world got to watch her ridiculousness. She wondered if it would help or hurt her sales.

"Hey," he said, squeezing her hand. "It was really brave, what you did. I'm proud of you."

She smiled back. It was nice to have him here, she thought, playing with the fingers on his hand. He had nice hands, strong hands, and that was comforting to her somehow.

He got a serious look on his face before he next spoke.

"You're getting out of here tomorrow, and Bill said he'd still be around and make sure you were OK. So how about next Saturday night? Dinner. Me and you."

Her curiosity about when he and Bill had gotten so close was halted by that. Was he asking her out again? "Like a date?" she asked, meeting his eyes, which were staring intensely at hers.

"Like a date," he agreed.

"Yes."

The smile on his face made her feel better than whatever drugs they had her on. Will wanted to go on a date with her. They could finally talk and get to the bottom of their issues. She'd finally be able to see if there was a way to work out whatever the problem was. Because working with him the last few days had confirmed it. Her feelings for Will hadn't gone anywhere, no matter how crazy he could make her. She sank back down into her pillows and got comfortable. A nap sounded like a great idea.

Will squeezed her hand again and leaned forward. He placed a soft kiss on her forehead before settling back down in his chair, still holding her hand.

That was nice.

CHAPTER THIRTY-FOUR

BETRAYAL IS THE ONLY TRUTH THAT STICKS

SITTING at the dim bar section in a fancy steakhouse, perched on a high stool, Cameron was loving life. They'd solved the crime, and her leg was healing. She'd spent the last week with Bill sharing her one-bedroom apartment while he "took care of her." As much as she loved him, it was nice to see him head back to Boston this morning. Her place just wasn't made for two people, and her frustration with his hovering and her healing leg made her a little more prickly than usual.

Things between her and Will were in a better place than they ever had been. They'd sent a few messages back and forth during the week. Their tone was light, fun, and flirty, which amped up her anticipation for tonight. She'd been looking forward to it all week. She'd taken a lot more time than she'd ever admit to anyone deciding what to wear, settling on a little black dress she'd had hanging in her closet waiting for an occasion to wear it for too long. She'd even taken time to do her makeup. Traditionally, she was a basic lip gloss and mascara kind of girl, but she'd gone all out for her date. She'd flat-ironed her long brown hair to a glossy shine and done a dark smokey eye that she thought made her look a bit exotic. She'd even gone for a bright red lipstick, which simultaneously boosted her confidence and gave her anxiety about getting it on her teeth. But she looked hot, so it was a win regardless.

To top it off, she had a dirty vodka martini with blue cheese olives in her hand, her favorite fancy drink and the one she ordered every time she went to a steakhouse. She even had a lead on a new client from the party and a call scheduled with Nate to maybe do some part-time work for him. It could be just what she needed to bring in some extra cash, and if she could finagle health insurance out of the deal, it would help to cut down her expenses. She still needed to get rid of the Jeep, but that was a problem for another day. Things were going well, and it was time to celebrate. Or they would celebrate if Will ever showed up; he was already a half an hour late.

She didn't really mind his tardiness. It gave her time to work up her nerve. She was going to take Phil's advice. She was going to have it out with Will about their issues and try to fix it. It really all boiled down to communication. They were both busy and stubborn, which wasn't a great combination. If this was going to work, they'd both need to make an effort. She was going to be brave and put her feelings out on the table. If this dinner invite was any indication, he was open to the idea.

She spun around in her chair and checked the quiet bar area again, looking for any sign of him. It was dead in the place, and the low lighting made it feel much later than six o'clock. There were only a few people in the bar with her, and looking them over again reassured her she hadn't missed Will. She turned back to the bar and her drink, resigned to waiting.

"Hey, baby, come here often?" The cheesy pickup line came from the right. She could feel someone slide into the barstool next to her.

"Listen, buddy," she said as she swung to face the idiot crowding her who'd have the nerve to try that old line. Holy. Shit. Her jaw dropped.

"Hey, Cameron. How are you?"

"Hello, Jack," she answered, stunned. "What the hell are you doing here?"

"Meeting a friend, you?"

"Oh, shit, I'm so sorry. I meant to be here earlier, but I got hung up at work," Will said as he came rushing up to them, dropping his head to place a kiss on Cameron's cheek. "Hey, Cam, so sorry. Jack."

Her brain screeched to a halt. Jack? Did they know each other?

"Hey, Will," the man on the barstool next to her answered, reaching out to shake his hand.

He flagged the bartender and was in the process of ordering them both drinks while her brain was spinning.

"You two know each other?" she stammered. It was all she could manage to get out, she was so stunned.

They shared a quick look, and Jack stuck his hand out to her.

"Jack Rosado, ATF. I'm an old army buddy of Will's."

She shook his hand numbly. Will had lied to her. And he had kept doing it. Every time she'd asked if he was looking into the case, he blew her off. He'd known exactly who Jack was. He knew the whole time.

"I'm sorry, Cameron. I couldn't tell you," Will said.

"That's my fault," Jack interjected, trying to take the heat off Will. "I needed your help, but we couldn't tell you why. It wasn't supposed to go down like that. You were supposed to help us, get your check, and go home none the wiser. But I messed up. I figured out what it was that tipped you off. I spelled Will's name wrong. A small error, but you're a sharp girl, and before I knew it, you were gone. I reached out to Will so he could take care of it on his end. I'm sorry for the deception, but we couldn't tell you until the case was over."

"And what was the case?" she asked calmly, sedate on the outside but seething inside.

"Guy jumped bail. He was a weapons dealer. Explosives mostly. They didn't think he was a flight risk because of his family, but he did a runner. We caught him yesterday. Thanks in part to your help. With the timeline you gave us, you allowed us to put together a good map of his movements. From that we were able to get camera footage from the neighborhood and track him down."

She thought his explanation over, unwilling to take

anything Jack said at face value. It did make sense. All the data she'd pulled for him would support that. She was looking at it like it was an abduction, but it fit the other way too. He turned off his cameras and alarm and snuck out in the middle of the night.

"So, it was all a lie? No kidnapping? No missing kids?" He nodded. "Then why were you meeting with Will's team in his office? And why come find me at the pub the other night? What did your bail jumper have to do with our case?" she asked. They had all lied to her. Jack, Will, Vanessa, and even Captain Lovett. She thought she was part of the team. But she wasn't. She was an outsider. Completely on her own, no matter how they used her when it suited their purpose.

"He was a big investor in Synergistic, and we've been looking for him for a while. He's a weapons trafficker. Mostly guns, but some explosives too. We got a tip he was in the New York area right around the time the connection between the fires and all the board members at Synergistic was made. We thought it might be him, because no one could determine how the fires were set. We thought it was possible we were looking at a new kind of explosive. By the time we made the connection to the townhouse in Brooklyn, he'd already left town. Will and I discussed it, and since he couldn't bring you in on his end, we thought you'd maybe be able to help us from our angle," Jack explained.

"Turned out to be nothing," Will said. "There was no connection. That's what Vanessa was working on the whole time. But there wasn't anything there. You figured out the real motive for the fires."

So," Jack said, draining the beer he'd ordered and standing up. He reached into his pocket and handed her an envelope. "I'm not here to crash your date. I'm just here to give you this."

"What's this?" she asked, taking it but not opening it.

"It's your consulting fee. Ten thousand dollars a day. I already paid you for Monday, but this covers the rest of the week." She just stared at him blankly. "You earned it," Jack said in answer to her hesitation.

She looked at the envelope in her hand. He had lied to her, manipulated her. Played on her emotions using a story that there were two missing children's lives at stake. It was despicable. He'd made her call her brother, and this was the hush money. Her breathing got heavy, and her skin hot. The same anger she had felt in Clint's office when she confronted Drew rolled over her and covered her vision in a haze.

Did this mean Will didn't really want to see her again? Was this just a fake date to get her here? Her heart sank at the thought.

Jack got up to shake Will's hand and leave, but before he could go, she stood up from the bar and turned to face the men.

She was on fire.

"Jack," she called, and when he turned her way, she swiftly shot her knee right up into his groin with all the strength she could manage. When he crumbled forward, she grabbed the back of his head and slammed it into her knee again. He fell to the sticky bar floor in a heap.

She came back from her daydream still sitting frozen at the bar. Jack had been calling her name. His hand reached out, and she shook it mechanically.

When she thought back, it wasn't the first time over the last week that she'd felt like this. She had been so quick to anger recently, felt so betrayed. If she was analytical about it, the reason was always Will. He had gone behind her back to Phil for help. He'd suspected her of a crime. He'd put her in the position to have to defend her life against a killer. Again. And then, he'd lied to her about Jack. The whole situation was still confusing to her, but she did know one thing. Nothing was worth feeling this kind of pain.

She sent Will a blistering look as she reached back to the bar, grabbed her drink, and drained it. Then, without another word, she grabbed her bag and walked away. She shoved the check inside as she moved toward the door.

"Cam," Will said. But she didn't break her stride. Just flipped them both the middle finger over her shoulder and pushed the door open and left.

Walking out onto the street and into the dimming sunlight felt like leaving a dark movie theater during the day, and she was temporarily blinded by the glare. She slid her sunglasses onto her face and set off down Lex at a brisk pace, anxious to just get away from all of it. From them.

She didn't need that kind of drama in her life. She was fine on her own. She had a great apartment, great friends, and her business was finally starting to come together. She didn't need a man to make her happy, especially one who jerked her around.

Fuck them both, she thought. Then she remembered the check in her bag and switched her destination to her bank. Well, on the bright side, at least she wouldn't need to worry about money for a while.

ACKNOWLEDGEMENTS

Big thanks to the crew at Hot Tree Self-publishing without who this would not be possible.

Thanks to my family, Mom, Dad, Andy, Kristen, Graham, Parker and our newest family member Bear.

To Ken and Ben, who let me turn them into such amazing characters. But if Ben doesn't stop with the Dad jokes, he won't be getting the all funny lines in the next book. Seriously, you have to stop.

To my NE team, Eytan, Jay, Scott, and Tayt. You guys make work fun. And the rest of the team at C4/SO who make all my days brighter.

To Clint and Drew who wanted to have their names in this book. Be careful what you wish for.

Nancy, who listens to, and supports all my book related drama.

My Friday night poker crew, I can't believe you wouldn't let me use the names of your businesses in the book but you're still cool.

And the AV Industry Media who have been so supportive

and amazing at helping me get my first book out to the industry. Kayte McGreggor Bennett, Tim Albright, Jeremy Glowacki, Ron Callis, and so many others.

To the AV Yoga group for being so supportive and inspiring, being around a group of women like you makes me push harder. When I grow up, I want to be you guys.

To the Women of Avixa who made me a book club selection. Thank you, that may have been the coolest thing that's ever happened to me. I'm overwhelmed by your support and all you do for the women of our industry.

Elizabeth Scozzari and all the other Beta Readers who gave such good feedback and made this story come together.

Everyone who's supported me through the process of writing these, I know you guys are getting sick of me talking about books, but to be fair you should all read more.

And again, to all my dealers, past, present and future, IT'S FICTION and per the beta readers, nobody wants to read stereo instructions so I had to edit some things you may think needed to be there for clarification. I'm aware of how it all really works.

Also, for legal reasons, don't try this at home.

ABOUT THE AUTHOR

Kat has worked for eighteen years in sales in the AV industry, her love for technology starting early with her first computer, a Commodore64 at age six. She loved it until she realized you could put a magnet to the screen and it made pretty colors.

Kat spends a lot of her time traveling. She's been to forty-six states and lived in six. She loves yoga, poker, sports, and all things technology. Her dreams are to one day stop travelling so much and be able to own a dog and to be the first woman to win the World Series of Poker Main Event.